Fragments of the Canvas Odyssey from Nottingha

Unveiling the Dark Strokes o

Preface

Life often presents us with canvases waiting to be painted, and within those strokes lie tales of beauty, crime, and the search for redemption. In "Fragments of the Canvas," John MacGregor's odyssey becomes a narrative brush, weaving together the ordinary and the extraordinary. As we delve into the fragments of his story, let us contemplate the complex portrait of a man navigating the twists and turns of fate, one shadowy stroke at a time.

Contents

Chapter 1: A Frosty Awakening

The cold tendrils of winter clung to the world outside as John MacGregor, a retired Royal Marine commando and ex-deep-sea diver, opened his eyes to a new day. The room was dimly lit by the pale light sneaking through the gaps in the curtains. His two faithful companions, Max and Bella, stirred from their slumber at the foot of the bed, their excitement palpable.

Rolling out of bed, John felt the chill of the room as he padded over to the window. A thick layer of frost painted the world outside, turning the fallen leaves into delicate sculptures. The breath of the morning lingered in the air, a visible reminder that winter had taken a firm grip.

John's mind, however, was not clouded by the cold. Retirement had brought with it a restlessness, a need for purpose that echoed through the corridors of his mind. The public school fees for his son, a place that represented opportunity and a chance at a different life, hung over him like a weight. His savings were not infinite, and he needed a way to supplement them.

As Max and Bella eagerly pranced around, John found solace in the routine of the morning walk. The crunch of frost beneath his boots and the brisk air filling his lungs cleared his mind. The dogs, sensing his anticipation, circled him like a pair of sentinels.

Returning home, John's breath hung in the air as he prepared for the day. His reflection in the mirror told tales of years spent in service, lines etched by experiences both fierce and tender. Today, though retired, a new mission awaited him – not one of combat, but a battle against the financial challenges that retirement brought.

Dressed in layers to combat the biting cold, John made his way to the front door, his loyal companions at his side. As he stepped out into the winter morning, the world outside seemed to pause for a moment, acknowledging the beginning of a new chapter.

The day ahead promised to be long and challenging, filled with the hustle and bustle of the holiday season. John, however, faced it with a sense of purpose. The uniform he now wore, that of a postman, symbolized a new direction in his life. Each step on his delivery route carried him closer to financial stability and the assurance that his son's education would continue uninterrupted.

With the dogs by his side, John set out into the frosty landscape, ready to embrace the day and the opportunities it held. The journey of the retired Royal Marine turned postman had just begun, and the pages of his new chapter were waiting to be written in the ink of determination and resilience.

Chapter 2: Battling Memories and Cold Limbs

The wooden floor of John's modest bedroom creaked under his weight as he sat down on the edge of the bed. His breath formed wisps in the air, a testament to the chill that had seeped into his bones. The battle-hardened hands that had once gripped the handles of a diving helmet now moved to his tired, bruised feet.

Barefoot, he examined the wear and tear of his soles, a map of bruises and callouses that told the story of miles covered in the pursuit of delivering letters and parcels. The cold had not been kind to his limbs, and the memories of past battles resurfaced with each twinge of pain.

His feet, once accustomed to the flinty sands of Qatar's oil fields and the frozen landscapes of Norway, now bore the scars of a different kind of warfare. Trench foot, a lingering spectre from the Falklands War, and the frostbite endured during 'Mountain and Arctic Warfare Training' haunted him in these frigid mornings.

John winced as he touched a particularly tender spot. The irony of the situation was not lost on him – a man who had once commanded a team of divers and ROV specialists now grappling with the aftermath of a day's walk through the streets of his town. The once pristine, unblemished feet that had navigated the depths of the ocean floor were now worn and battered by the simple act of delivering mail.

Despite the physical toll, a different battle waged within him. The frustration of being accustomed to a world where experience and expertise were revered clashed with the reality of a civilian job where the word 'seniority' was wielded by those with fewer years under their belts than he had served in the military.

In the silence of the room, memories flooded back – the distant echoes of a younger man navigating the icy waters off Norway and the adrenaline-fueled days in the Falklands. Now, in his fifties, the years seemed to pile on like the snow outside his window.

Yet, he refused to surrender to the pain or the indignity. The urge to tell the managers where to shove the job had flirted with the edge of his resolve, but he held back. Pride, the same pride that had seen him through war zones, swelled within him. He wouldn't be beaten, not by the cold, the physical strain, or the whims of younger superiors.

With a determined breath, he reached for his socks and boots. Each movement, a quiet act of defiance against the pain and the memories. The retired Royal Marine commando, now a postman, would not yield. As he laced up his boots, the chill of the morning seemed to seep away, replaced by the warmth of resilience and the unwavering spirit that had defined his entire life. The second chapter of this new journey had begun, etched in the quiet battle between pain and pride.

Chapter 3: A Parcel and Unexpected Encounters

The morning pressed on, and John trudged through the snowy landscape, a determined silhouette against the backdrop of winter. The weight of the parcels seemed to grow with each step, and the icy pavements added an unwelcome challenge to his mission. "This is no job for old men," he mumbled under his breath, feeling the strain on his bruised feet.

The frosty air bit at his face as he navigated the maze of streets, his breath visible in the chill. The parcels, stacked high in his mailbag, tugged at his weary shoulders. Yet, amidst the physical struggle, there was a glimmer of anticipation when he spotted the familiar address – Number 22 Bramble Drive.

A small smile crept across John's face as he thought of the young woman who awaited her deliveries with a certain playful charm. Her suggestive comments and flirtatious banter had become a welcome distraction from the challenges of the job. As he approached her door, holding up the parcel for the obligatory delivery photo, he couldn't help but feel a lift in his spirits.

He knocked on the door, the sound echoing through the quiet street. The anticipation grew, and he couldn't help but chuckle at the thought of her usual playful remarks. The door creaked open, revealing Number 22 Bramble Drive.

To John's surprise, the young woman stood before him, her bathrobe loosely tied around her waist, a mischievous smile playing on her lips. The unexpected sight caught him off guard, and for a moment, he struggled to find words.

"Special delivery," he managed to stammer, holding up the parcel for the customary photo. The young woman, undeterred by her choice of attire, giggled and leaned in slightly, her eyes sparkling with amusement.

"I thought I'd make your chilly day a bit warmer," she teased, her tone carrying a subtle wink. John, a seasoned veteran of both war and workplace politics, couldn't help but blush beneath the weathered lines of his face.

As he handed over the parcel, the young woman's laughter followed him down the path. The unexpected encounter left John both amused and slightly flustered. The weight of the parcels, the cold, and the icy paths seemed to momentarily dissipate, replaced by the warmth of an unexpected and slightly flirtatious exchange.

With a renewed sense of purpose, John continued his rounds, the memory of the encounter lingering like a small flame in the winter air. The retired Royal Marine commando pressed on, navigating the challenges of the job, each step a testament to the resilience that defined not just his military career but also this new chapter in his life as a postman.

Chapter 4: Nostalgia and Unexpected Encounters

The snowflakes danced from the sky, a soft flurry that painted the landscape in a pristine white. Christmas decorations adorned the housing estates, transforming the streets into a festive wonderland. For John, this sight held a special significance, reminiscent of the childhood Christmases he remembered from the 70s.

As he walked through the neighbourhoods of Saint Anns in Nottingham, the decorations, the twinkling lights, and the sense of community struck a chord deep within him. It was a stark contrast to the grandeur of public-school fees and the life he had known as a Royal Marine. Here, in the heart of a working-class neighbourhood, Christmas was celebrated with an authenticity and warmth that felt like a balm to his restless soul.

The houses, though modest, were adorned with an array of lights and decorations, each telling a story of effort and dedication. The nostalgia swept over John as he marvelled at the simple yet profound displays of holiday spirit. It was a scene he hadn't witnessed since he was a little boy, and the genuine joy of the community touched him in a way he hadn't expected.

Amidst the snow-covered streets, he continued his deliveries, his mailbag a sturdy companion against the winter chill. As he approached a well-lit house, he pressed the doorbell, the sound echoing through the festive air. The door opened, revealing a large woman who bent down to corral her enthusiastic dog.

In that moment, time seemed to slow. John's gaze unintentionally caught a longer-than-necessary glimpse of the ample cleavage on display. He quickly averted his eyes, a flush of embarrassment warming his cheeks. A subtle internal debate unfolded – was it a deliberate display, or a mere accident of circumstance?

Walking away, John couldn't shake the unexpected arousal that lingered. The juxtaposition of the festive surroundings and the spontaneous encounter left him contemplative. In a world where he battled the cold, the memories, and the challenges of a new job, the unpredictability of human interactions added a layer of complexity to his days.

As the snow continued to fall, settling on the decorated houses and the quiet streets of Saint Anns, John found himself navigating not only the physical obstacles but also the uncharted territory of his own emotions. The retired Royal Marine commando pressed on, his footsteps leaving a trail in the snow, each one marking a step in this intricate dance between the past and the present.

Chapter 5: Navigating the Labyrinth

As the winter day waned, the sun dipped below the horizon, casting long shadows on the snow-covered streets of Saint Anns. Determination filled John as he approached the remainder of his deliveries, each one akin to a mission in the intricate labyrinth of the housing estates.

In his mind, he summoned the resilience gained during his days at Lympstone Commando Training Centre, the gruelling assault course vivid in his memory. The labyrinth of St Anns, with its narrow side streets and hidden corners, resembled the Tarzan course, demanding a blend of strategic thinking and physical prowess.

The little streets posed challenges, much like the obstacles on the assault course. Some were narrow, requiring deft navigation, while others were steep, demanding an extra push against the winter incline. The parcels, like the tasks on the Tarzan course, required a methodical approach to ensure they reached their destination efficiently.

As the day turned into evening and the dim glow of streetlights replaced the fading sunlight, a new psychological factor entered the equation. The darkness brought with it a sense of urgency, a reminder that time was of the essence. Yet, John, drawing from the mental fortitude ingrained in him through years of military training, embraced the challenge.

He recalled the words of his training instructors echoing in his mind, "It's just a state of mind, MacGregor. The physical obstacles are nothing compared to the strength within." With each parcel delivered and every obstacle overcome, the labyrinth of St Anns became a mental battleground, and John was determined to emerge victorious.

The memories of Lympstone, the assault course, and the Tarzan course fueled his resolve. He moved through the maze of streets with the precision of a well-trained commando, his mind sharp, his steps purposeful. The Christmas lights that adorned the houses and the glow of the streetlights cast an ethereal ambiance, creating a stark contrast to the challenges he faced.

As he pressed on through the darkness, John knew that, like the commando tests of his youth, this too was a test of his mettle. The retired Royal Marine commando embraced the challenge with the same spirit that had seen him through the most demanding terrains and situations.

In the quiet of the night, with snow underfoot and the labyrinth of St Anns conquered, John reflected on the parallels between the military training of his past and the challenges of his present. The echoes of Lympstone guided him through the complex dance of streets, obstacles, and time. With a determined spirit, he cracked on, each step a testament to the resilience instilled in him by years of training and a lifetime of facing challenges head-on.

Chapter 6: Unseen Intricacies on Honeywood Drive

Honeywood Drive lay draped in the wintry darkness as John maneuvered his compact Fiat post van through the labyrinthine roads of St Anns. The festive lights that adorned the houses now seemed dim in the presence of a police van, strategically positioned with bold lettering proclaiming it as part of the 'Tactical Support Team.' Its flashing lights painted an eerie glow on the snow-covered pavement.

As John approached, he found his path blocked, or rather, semi-blocked, by the imposing presence of the police van. Tactical support teams were not an everyday sight in a neighbourhood like this, and curiosity mingled with caution in John's mind. The men inside, clad in civilian clothes with police vests identifying their affiliation, appeared engrossed in a discussion, their faces etched with a seriousness that hinted at unseen intricacies.

Determined to fulfil his duty, John deftly circumvented the police van, parking his little Fiat post van in its usual position. The parcels stacked in the back seemed to carry a weight beyond their physical form, as if mirroring the unspoken tension on Honeywood Drive.

Embarking on his walk deliveries along the quiet street, John couldn't help but steal glances toward the police van. The echoes of his past experiences, particularly his days on nuclear escorts, resonated as he observed the tactical support team. The men inside, seemingly engrossed in a mission known only to them, evoked memories of clandestine operations and heavy armaments.

In his days escorting nuclear materials, John had driven through the roads of Britain, his van laden with the weight of responsibility and the burden of knowledge hidden from the public. The connection between then and now was palpable. The 'cowboys,' as John quietly labelled them in his thoughts, were like shadowy figures from his past, men operating in a realm not readily visible to the average citizen.

He continued his walk, carefully placing parcels at each doorstep, the snow crunching beneath his boots. The festive lights that once symbolized warmth now flickered in the backdrop of police activity. John's gaze occasionally met with those of the tactical support team, the unspoken understanding between them acknowledging a different kind of duty being performed.

As he moved down Honeywood Drive, the night whispered secrets of unseen intricacies, reminding John that beneath the surface of the quiet neighbourhood, life unfolded in unpredictable ways. The retired Royal Marine commando, once a guardian of secrets, pressed on with his own mission, the parcels in his hands carrying not just gifts but the weight of experience and the resilience of a lifetime spent navigating the complexities of duty.

Chapter 7: A Welcome Reprieve

The night air clung to John's weary bones as he continued his rounds along Honeywood Drive. The chill had seeped through his layers, and even the resilient spirit of a Royal Marine couldn't entirely shield him from the biting cold. The allure of the warm glow emanating from the houses became increasingly tempting, and the invitation he least expected came from one doorstep.

A single mother, her house adorned with twinkling lights and a wreath on the door, greeted him with a warm smile. The connection between neighbours in a tight-knit community like St Anns often extended beyond mere pleasantries. Today, it offered a brief respite from the frigid night.

"You must be freezing out there. Why don't you come in for a moment, warm yourself up?" she suggested, her eyes reflecting genuine concern.

John hesitated for a moment, his commitment to finishing his rounds battling against the numbing cold. Yet, the allure of the cozy interior proved irresistible. With a grateful nod, he accepted the invitation, stepping into the warmth that enveloped him like a comforting embrace.

The single mother, whose name was Angela, led him into the living room where a crackling fire provided both light and warmth. The contrast between the freezing night and the toasty interior was like a shock to John's system, and he couldn't help but feel an overwhelming sense of gratitude.

As Angela disappeared into the kitchen to make a cup of tea, John took in the surroundings. The room was adorned with the simple beauty of holiday decorations, a modest tree twinkling in the corner. The soft glow cast a warm hue over the scene, creating an ambiance of coziness and festive cheer.

Angela returned with a steaming cup of tea, her eyes glinting with kindness. "You're doing a wonderful job out there. I thought you could use a little break," she said, her smile adding to the room's already inviting atmosphere.

The conversation flowed easily as they sipped tea, sharing snippets of their lives. Angela, a resilient single mother, spoke of the challenges she faced, and John, in turn, shared tales of his military adventures and the new challenges of his postman role. The warmth of the room extended beyond the crackling fire, wrapping around them like a comforting blanket.

As the teacups were emptied, Angela stood up, a mischievous twinkle in her eye. "You've been out in the cold long enough. How about we turn up the heat a bit?" she suggested, and with a playful grin, she adjusted the thermostat.

The room became warmer, but not just because of the rising temperature. Angela's subtle advances and the shared warmth of the moment created an unexpected and intimate connection. The cold outside seemed to vanish in the steam rising from the teacups and the newfound warmth between two strangers brought together by circumstance.

Feeling rejuvenated and with a smile that seemed to defy the winter night, John bid Angela farewell. The cold air outside felt less harsh, and the remaining parcels in his hands seemed lighter. As he continued his rounds through St Anns, the memory of that unexpected break lingered, making it a day that went down in his book as the perfect day for a postman.

The lights of Honeywood Drive twinkled in the distance, and John couldn't help but marvel at the unpredictable turns a day could take. The retired Royal Marine commando, now a postman, pressed on with a newfound energy, the warmth from Angela's home echoing in his steps as he navigated the quiet streets, each doorstep a reminder of the diverse and often surprising facets of the human experience.

Chapter 8: A Steamy Fantasy

The remnants of warmth from Angela's house accompanied John as he continued his rounds through St Anns. The cold had lost some of its bite, replaced by the lingering glow of shared moments and unexpected connections. Yet, as he navigated the snow-covered streets, a different kind of warmth kindled within him.

The images of Angela's living room, the crackling fire, and the intimate conversation replayed in John's mind. A certain mischievous twinkle in Angela's eye lingered, sparking a flame of desire. He couldn't help but indulge in a fantasy—a steamy romp between the sheets that went beyond the boundaries of the cups of tea they had shared.

In his mental reverie, John, a man seasoned by three marriages and experiences in various corners of the world, imagined showing Angela the expertise of a man who had loved and been loved in countries as diverse as Thailand, Singapore, China, and the Americas. The knowledge he had gained over the years about what women desire in the throes of passion painted vivid scenes in his imagination.

The steamy fantasy unfolded like a novel, each mental image a chapter that went beyond the snowy landscapes of St Anns. Angela, with her warm smile and inviting eyes, became the protagonist in this private tale, and John, the experienced lover, guided her through the intricacies of desire.

The mental escapade, though intense, was tempered by the reality of his role as a postman, the parcels in his hands acting as anchors to the present. The cold air outside, the crunch of snow beneath his boots, and the responsibility of his job pulled him back from the heated reverie.

As he delivered parcels to the remaining houses on his route, John couldn't shake the lingering warmth of his fantasy. The dichotomy between the professional postman and the passionate lover played out in his mind. Each knock on a door, each interaction with a resident, became a reminder of the diverse roles one could inhabit in a single day.

The fantasy fuelled John's steps, adding a subtle swagger to his walk as he made his way through St Anns. The intimate moments in his imagination mingled with the reality of the quiet neighbourhood, creating a complex tapestry of emotions and desires.

As he approached the end of his rounds, the snow-covered streets bore witness to the dichotomy within John – the disciplined postman and the man who had lived a life rich with experiences. The glow of Angela's home, both in reality and in fantasy, added a layer of complexity to this chilly winter day. The retired Royal Marine commando, now a postman with a trove of memories, pressed on, each step a dance between the practical and the passionate, the known and the imagined.

Chapter 9: Nostalgic Readings and Present-Day Innuendos

As John made his way through the wintry streets of St Anns, the echoes of Angela's warmth and the lingering images of his steamy fantasy accompanied him like silent companions. The desire for a break from the chill led him to reminisce about his past, particularly his school days in the 70s. A particular book sprang to mind—one he had read as a young lad with a curious mind: 'Confessions of a Postman.'

Intrigued by the memories it brought back, John decided to revisit the book. Thanks to the wonders of modern technology, he swiftly Googled the title and, with a few clicks, found himself the proud owner of a copy. The nostalgia of flipping through the pages of a book from his youth filled him with a sense of anticipation.

As he delved into the tales of a fellow postman's experiences, the pages unfolded a world of anecdotes, humour, and perhaps a bit of embellishment. The stories resonated with John, and each turn of the page brought back memories of his own journey as a postman—a retired Royal Marine commando navigating the intricacies of a new civilian life.

Some chapters elicited laughter, while others triggered a twinge of recognition. The world of mail delivery, it seemed, was a tapestry of unique encounters and unexpected moments. John found solace in the shared experiences of postmen across different eras, realizing that the innuendos and playful banter from recipients were not unique to his time alone.

A particular section of the book talked about the subtle flirtations and suggestive comments that postmen often encountered. The stories mirrored the playful interactions John had experienced himself—moments like "Oh, it's too big for my box, is it?" and the classic "While you're down there!" that never failed to elicit a smile.

The realization that such encounters were timeless brought forth a sense of connection to postmen of the past. The innuendos, it seemed, were a part of the job, a universal constant that transcended generations. The book became a mirror reflecting not only the light-hearted moments of the job but also the camaraderie and shared experiences that made being a postman a unique and often entertaining profession.

As John closed the book, he couldn't help but feel a renewed appreciation for his role. The anecdotes and memories, whether from the 70s or his current days in St Anns, added depth to the layers of his journey. The retired Royal Marine commando, who had weathered wars and navigated the complexities of love and duty, now found fulfilment in the simple joys and shared smiles of his postman adventures.

With a contented sigh, John continued his rounds, the book tucked under his arm. The wintry air seemed to carry not just the chill of the night but also the warmth of shared stories and the timeless charm of being a postman. The echoes of 'Confessions of a Postman' lingered as he approached each doorstep, a reminder that, in the world of mail delivery, some things remained delightfully unchanged.

Chapter 10: Anticipation Amidst the Chill

The morning light struggled to pierce through the thick clouds, signalling that the day ahead promised more than just a nip in the air. As John prepared for another round of deliveries through the snowy streets of St Anns, he couldn't help but glance out the window at the impending snowfall. The weather report suggested a day of snow and ice, a prospect that threatened to dampen the enthusiasm he had carried through the previous rounds.

The prospect of facing the biting cold and treacherous icy paths weighed on John's mind. The wintry conditions posed a challenge that even the resilient Royal Marine couldn't entirely shake off. Yet, as he zipped up his coat and stepped into the frosty morning, a different kind of warmth began to build within him—a warmth not derived from layers of clothing or the blazing sun but from the anticipation of a particular encounter.

One of the women on his round, a resident whose doorstep he would soon be visiting, had a way of adding a spark to his day. The thought of the warmth of another body, the shared smiles, and the brief yet meaningful conversations fuelled him with a unique energy. It wasn't just the physical warmth he craved on this chilly day; it was the emotional connection, the brief moments of human interaction that made the rounds more than just a job.

As John walked through the snow-covered streets, each step felt purposeful, driven by the anticipation of that meeting. The crunch of snow beneath his boots seemed to echo the rhythm of his own heartbeat, a steady cadence of excitement. The snowflakes, though cold as they landed on his face, couldn't extinguish the warmth building within him.

The prospect of sharing a moment with someone on his route transformed the mundane into the extraordinary. The snowy backdrop, the quiet streets, and the impending encounter became elements of a story yet to unfold. The winter chill was momentarily forgotten as the anticipation of connection took centre stage.

With each doorstep approached, John couldn't help but wonder if the encounter he anticipated would unfold as he hoped. The unpredictability of these moments added a layer of excitement to his routine. The resilience that had seen him through wars and icy waters now propelled him forward, driven by the warmth of shared moments that awaited.

As the snow began to fall, John pressed on through the labyrinth of St Anns. The wintry weather outside seemed inconsequential compared to the warmth building within him. The retired Royal Marine commando, now a postman, found solace in the anticipation of the human connections waiting for him amidst the snowflakes and icy pavements. The day ahead, despite its challenges, held the promise of shared warmth, making the journey through St Anns not just a job but a series of moments that made the chill of winter bearable.

Chapter 11: A Snowy Morning's Resolve

The morning sun cast a gentle glow on the snow-covered streets of St Anns, transforming the night into a winter wonderland. As the clubs closed, students spilled out onto the snow-covered pavements, delighting in impromptu snowball fights. The crisp air echoed with laughter and the soft thud of snowballs hitting their targets.

For John, the snowy morning held a different charm. The night had left the world draped in white, the sky bright with the promise of a new day. His two dogs, Sumo and Teddy, revelled in the snow, their paws leaving fresh imprints in the virgin snow. Teddy, at just four months old, experienced the snow for the first time, his playful antics adding a touch of innocence to the wintry scene.

As he watched his dogs prance and dance in the snow, John's thoughts turned to the day's tasks. The narrow streets of St Anns posed a challenge, especially when blanketed in snow. The gritters, with their salt and grit, wouldn't be making their way through these narrow passages. Cars, parked tightly on either side, further narrowed the already challenging roads.

The idea of navigating these wintry streets, considering the potential hazards, flickered in John's mind. The responsibility of his job, the commitment to delivering the mail, fought against the inclination to take a snow day. The thought crossed his mind to call it a day, to retreat from the snowy streets and let the weather dictate a break.

However, the echoes of a work ethic forged in his youth, a determination that persisted from his days as a schoolboy delivering newspapers, won over. Memories of Lower Bagthorpe, the long farmhouses with even longer driveways, flashed in his mind. Back then, he faced the challenges of delivering papers in the rain and wind, a commitment to completing the round and delivering the news to every doorstep.

The figure of 'Nora Batty,' the shop owner from whom he collected papers at 5 o'clock every morning, loomed in his memories. The long, three-mile round along Lower Bagthorpe, with its scattered farmhouses and challenging driveways, instilled a sense of discipline and determination. It was a lesson that transcended the decades.

Just as he had resolved to finish the newspaper round despite the weather, John decided to press on with his postman duties. The thought of letting people down, even in the face of snow-covered obstacles, fuelled his determination. The work ethic cultivated in the early hours of a paper round, half a century ago, remained alive and well within him.

As he geared up for the day ahead, the snow-covered streets of St Anns awaited. The retired Royal Marine commando, now a postman with decades of experience, would once again brave the wintry conditions, each step in the snow a testament to a work ethic that withstood the test of time.

Chapter 12: A Slippery Encounter

The snow-laden streets of Bramble Avenue glistened in the morning light as John navigated his way through the wintry maze. The chill in the air hinted at the challenges that awaited him, but the resilient postman pressed on, determined to fulfil his duty. Little did he know that the icy conditions had a surprise in store for him, right outside the familiar doorstep of Number 22.

As he approached, a sudden slip on an icy patch sent him tumbling to the ground, his parcels scattered in the snow. A moment of awkwardness and surprise gripped him, but before he could fully process the situation, the door of Number 22 swung open. The woman who always received a parcel from him, with a warm smile and playful banter, rushed outside.

"Are you okay? Any injuries?" she asked, genuine concern etched on her face. Her hands instinctively ran over his body, checking for signs of harm. The unexpected tumble had left him momentarily stunned, but the warmth of her concern began to thaw the chill.

"Come inside, let's have a look," she insisted, guiding him into her house. The contrast between the cold exterior and the warmth within was palpable. John, still trying to shake off the shock of the fall, couldn't believe his luck. What were the chances of slipping right on her doorstep?

Once inside, she insisted he take off his wet clothes to prevent catching a cold. "I'll get you some dry stuff while we dry yours," she said, disappearing into another room. John found himself standing in her cozy hallway, surrounded by the comforting warmth of her home.

As she returned with dry clothes, John couldn't help but appreciate the unexpected turn of events. Stripping off his wet clothes right there in front of her, he revealed more than just his vulnerability. The act of undressing, in the intimacy of her home, laid bare a different kind of connection between them.

She handled the situation with a blend of professionalism and empathy. The dry clothes she handed him were not just garments; they were symbols of a shared moment. As she took his wet clothes to be dried, her gaze lingered, and John sensed a spark of something more than mere kindness.

In the midst of the snow-covered morning, in the warmth of her home, John experienced a unique blend of vulnerability and connection. The unexpected slip on the icy doorstep had led to a situation that went beyond the realms of a typical postman's day. As she expertly massaged his muscles, the lines between professionalism and something more blurred, leaving John to ponder the twists and turns that life, like the snowy streets of Bramble Avenue, could take.

Chapter 13: The Weight of Tomorrow's Worries

In the quiet moments of his Sunday, John found himself wrestling with the familiar companions of anxiety and anticipation. Despite the day being designated as his time off, a paradox unfolded within him. His mind, wired with meticulous precision from years of military training and commercial diving, couldn't quite switch off the planning mechanism.

He had read books advocating the philosophy of "Don't sweat the small stuff," and yet, the small stuff seemed to hold an inexplicable allure for his thoughts. Every Sunday became a mental battleground, a clash between the desire to relax and the compulsion to anticipate the challenges of the week ahead.

The anxiety crept in stealthily, manifesting in the form of questions that echoed in his mind: What should he wear tomorrow? What would the weather be like? Which footwear would be most suitable for the day's tasks? These seemingly inconsequential details became the protagonists of his Sunday, each one vying for attention in the theatre of his thoughts.

While the world outside his window slept peacefully under the serene Sunday sky, John's mind buzzed with the hum of planning and worry. The paradox lay in the fact that, come Monday, when the day's challenges unfurled before him, the weight of these worries seemed to dissipate like morning mist.

In the practical realm of his postman duties, the meticulous planning transformed into a seamless execution. What to wear, how to navigate the streets, and the intricacies of weather considerations became secondary to the rhythmic dance of delivering mail. The worries that had loomed large on Sunday now seemed like inconspicuous shadows in the light of actual performance.

It was as if the act of doing, the engagement with the task at hand, held a magical quality that dissipated the anxieties of anticipation. Each delivery, each step along the familiar streets, brought a sense of ease that defied the meticulous planning that had preceded it.

John found solace in this paradox, recognizing the quirk in his own nature. The worry that accompanied Sunday's planning sessions seemed almost disproportionate when juxtaposed with the calm efficiency he demonstrated during his postman duties. The small stuff that had occupied his thoughts lost its significance in the face of tangible action.

As Sunday gently transitioned into Monday, John knew that the worries would resurface, that the meticulous planning for the next challenge would commence once again. Yet, with the experience of countless Mondays behind him, he embraced the paradox with a knowing smile. The weight of tomorrow's worries, he realized, was a mere illusion, dissolving like snowflakes on a warm palm when confronted with the reality of the present moment.

Chapter 14: Raindrops and Reserved Reflections

The morning sky wept, as raindrops tap-danced on the windowpanes, heralding a wet start to the day. John, always attuned to the nuances of weather, faced the soggy reality during the first walk of the day with his dogs. The rain, a persistent companion, had a peculiar way of bringing tranquillity to his thoughts. The rhythmic pitter-patter seemed to align with the measured cadence of his own contemplations.

As he mulled over the day ahead, a decision crystallized in his mind. Today, he would forego the convenience of his trusty van and opt for a walk down to the sorting office on Lower Parliament

Street. The thought of avoiding the inevitable quest for a parking space later on sealed the deal. The rain, with its cathartic drumming on the pavement, felt like a fitting backdrop to this decision.

Unlike the animated conversations that unfolded within the sorting office, John's interactions with his new workmates were minimal. A quick nod or a crisp "Good morning" sufficed to acknowledge their shared space. He wasn't antisocial; rather, he had spent the majority of his life in roles that didn't require constant verbal exchange. The precision of his military background and the focused solitude of deep-sea diving had forged a quiet demeanour.

Within the sorting office, as his colleagues engaged in the morning banter, John immersed himself in marking down house numbers on his pre-prepared list. Each parcel had its designated spot, a system meticulously crafted for efficiency. The steady strokes of his pen across the paper echoed the certainty with which he approached his daily tasks.

It wasn't that John was averse to socializing; he simply found comfort in the solitude of his routines. The quiet conversations he shared with the parcels on his list served as a form of communication that felt familiar and natural. As he made his way through the sorting office, his eyes and mind absorbed the information around him, registering the details needed for the day's deliveries.

The rain, now a steady companion to his journey, added a layer of serenity to his thoughts. Each step towards Lower Parliament Street felt purposeful, a deliberate stride through the wet streets of Nottingham. The umbrella, an unassuming shield against the raindrops, became an extension of his determined presence.

As John embraced the wet morning with the stoic resolve he carried from his military days, he knew that the day's challenges awaited. The sorting office, a bustling microcosm of activity, pulsed with energy as parcels were sorted and routes planned. In the midst of it all, John found a rhythm that complemented the cadence of raindrops, a quiet reflection in the midst of a downpour, preparing for another day of delivering amidst the small talk and silent efficiency of the postman's world.

Chapter 15: The Echo of a Cinematic Ring

As John walked through the rain-soaked streets, an unexpected phrase echoed in his mind, "The Postman Always Rings Twice." The connection was distant, a thread from the tapestry of old films, a 1946 noir classic. He couldn't quite pinpoint why this particular movie title had surfaced in his thoughts, but the whims of his mind often led him down uncharted paths.

The phrase lingered, a peculiar mantra that accompanied him as he navigated the wet labyrinth of Nottingham's neighbourhoods. While the title was rooted in a film noir plot, its resonance in his mind took on a different nuance. To John, the "Postman Always Rings Twice" became a whimsical reminder, a mental motif that injected a touch of intrigue into the routine of his deliveries.

The mundane act of delivering mail, though systematic and efficient, was not immune to the whimsy of John's offbeat mind. The phrase, borrowed from the cinematic realm, transformed his daily rounds into a subtle dance of anticipation and surprise. As he approached each doorstep, the echo of the postman ringing twice lingered, a nod to the unpredictable nature of human interactions.

John found solace in these subtle diversions. The routine, while defined by precision and order, was not devoid of moments that transcended the ordinary. The strange off-the-track musings of his mind became a form of mental choreography, turning the act of delivering mail into a performance that embraced the unexpected.

As the rain continued to fall, the echoes of the cinematic phrase blended with the rhythmic pattering of raindrops on his umbrella. The streets of Nottingham, adorned with reflections of city lights in the wet pavement, became a cinematic backdrop to his own narrative. Each house, each parcel, held the potential for a twist in the plot, a moment that deviated from the script of the ordinary.

The idea that the postman always rings twice, while rooted in film noir allure, became a metaphor for John's approach to his daily rounds. It was a reminder that in the seemingly routine and predictable, there existed room for nuance, for the unexpected ring of connection that could transform an ordinary encounter into a memorable scene.

And so, under the rainy Nottingham sky, John continued his journey. The phrase, a whimsical companion, added a layer of intrigue to the act of delivering mail. In the world of routine and structure, his offbeat mind danced with the echoes of cinematic nostalgia, turning the ordinary into a canvas for the extraordinary.

Chapter 16: Echoes of Rain, Shadows of War

The relentless rain drummed on the windows; each drop a haunting echo that reverberated through John's mind. Yesterday's cold, wet downpour had triggered a cascade of memories, unlocking a door he preferred to keep firmly closed. The cloak of Post Traumatic Stress Disorder (PTSD) enveloped him, its weight pressing on his shoulders as he navigated through the present, tethered to the shadows of his past.

The rain in Nottingham, mirroring the relentless showers in the Falklands decades ago, became an unwitting accomplice in resurrecting memories John had long sought to bury. The Falklands War of 1982, a chapter etched in the recesses of his mind, unfolded before him with vivid clarity. Stepping off the landing craft into the icy Atlantic waters, the frigid embrace soaked him to the bone, sealing his fate in the unforgiving cold for the next six weeks.

The wind, a constant companion in the Falklands, was a relentless force, adding a cruel "wind-chill" factor to the already numbing cold. The rain, a horizontal assault, mimicked the downpour in Nottingham, knitting the past and present together in an unexpected dance of torment.

Yesterday's rain wasn't just water; it was a portal to a time when the elements were not just an inconvenience but a relentless adversary. The cold, creeping into his bones, had become synonymous with his nemesis—water. A cruel reminder of frostbite and trench foot, afflictions that never truly released their grip on his extremities.

Today, as the rain continued its melancholic symphony, John felt the burden of depression settling in, a storm cloud that mirrored the one outside. His hands, once battered by the biting cold of the Falklands, throbbed with phantom pains. The spectre of PTSD cast a long shadow, leaving him vulnerable to the invisible wounds that lingered beneath the surface.

His mood, usually buoyant and resilient, wavered in the face of this unwelcome visitation from the past. The raindrops seemed to trace the contours of his memories, painting a canvas of desolation. He needed something, a lifeline to pull him from the undertow of despair.

And so, in the face of the looming tempest, John grasped for his mantra. "I do wonderful work in a wonderful way; I give wonderful service for wonderful pay!" The words, a lifeline of positivity, became his anchor against the rising tide of darkness. He chanted them with a fervour born from necessity, each syllable a shield against the encroaching shadows.

As he readied himself for another day of confronting the rain and the demons it summoned, John clung to his mantra, a beacon of light in the storm. The relentless patter of raindrops outside would not drown out the echo of his own resilient chant, a counterbalance to the haunting memories that threatened to engulf him. In the quiet recitation of his mantra, John found a thread of hope to guide him through the wet and miserable day that lay ahead, both in Nottingham and within the tempest of his own mind.

Chapter 17: A Ray of Sunshine

As the grey sky began to fracture, allowing rays of sunlight to pierce through the persistent clouds, an unexpected warmth seeped into John's spirits. The sudden shift in weather mirrored the internal transformation within him. The rain, which had felt like a relentless assault, now glistened on the leaves like diamonds, a testament to the transient nature of storms.

With each step, the weight of depression lifted, and the shadows of the past receded like a retreating tide. The sunlit patches on the wet pavement were an invitation to embrace the present, and John found himself captivated by the beauty of the post-rain world.

As he approached each doorstep, a subtle shift occurred. People, sensing the change in his demeanour, greeted him with a warmth that mirrored the newfound sunlight. "Are you warm enough, love?" they asked, genuine concern replacing the casual exchanges. John, for a moment, felt the embrace of community, a connection forged not just by shared spaces but by shared vulnerabilities.

He couldn't help but smile at the simplicity of human kindness. The mundane conversations on the doorsteps became a lifeline, pulling him further from the edge of melancholy. The weight of age, a burden he carried like a weary traveller, seemed to ease as the community reached out with words of concern and camaraderie.

During these small interactions, John's perspective shifted. This, he realized, was not just a job for "Old Men," as he had mused earlier. Age brought with it a different kind of richness—an experiential wealth that resonated with those around him. The unexpected invite into Number 22, with its promise of shared stories and warmth, became a testament to the value of experience.

As he entered the cozy living room of Number 22, the contrast between the cold and wet outdoors and the inviting indoors was palpable. The warmth enveloped him, both physically and metaphorically. The lushes' single mother, with her playful banter and expert massage, reminded him that experiences were not confined to the distant past—they could be woven into the fabric of the present.

The depression that had loomed like a heavy cloud had dissipated, replaced by the warmth of human connection and the unexpected joys that life, much like the weather, could bring. John, with a renewed sense of purpose, continued his rounds. The sunlit interludes between the clouds were not just a meteorological phenomenon; they reflected the resilience of the human spirit. The postman, once burdened by the shadows of war and weather, now embraced the unfolding day with a newfound appreciation for the sunshine that breaks through even the darkest clouds.

Chapter 18: The Magpies' Omen

The morning unfolded with a peculiar twist of fate as John embarked on his walk with the dogs. Two magpies, their sleek black and white plumage catching the morning light, danced on the path ahead. It was a sight that, to many, might seem trivial, but John, ever attuned to the rhythms of superstition, recited the age-old ditty in his mind, "One for sorrow, two for joy." A silly superstition, perhaps, but it brought a smile to his face and set the tone for the day.

Wednesday, the notorious hump day, loomed ahead, consistent in its reputation as the most challenging day for parcels and mail. Yet, armed with the notion that the magpies had promised a day of joy, John steeled himself with positivity. "It's only a state of mind," he mused, a mantra that had become his anchor in the turbulent seas of postal chaos.

Before venturing into the sorting office, a robust English breakfast fortified him for the day's challenges. The clatter and chaos of the sorting office were an inevitable prelude to the day's deliveries. The morning routine unfolded in a frenetic symphony of voices, shouts, and the persistent hum of sorting machines.

As the parcels were allocated, the tension in the sorting office escalated. The bitter rivalry over who had the heaviest load reached a crescendo at 07:45, a prelude to the battles that lay ahead on the streets of Nottingham. Two colleagues, caught in the crossfire of allocation disputes, nearly came to blows. The banter, once light-hearted, had morphed into a powder keg of misdirected frustration.

Outside, two colleagues taking a smoke break couldn't resist commenting on John's distinctive wax hat. "Going fishing, mate?" one of them quipped. John, accustomed to the ribbing but feeling the edge of irritation, shot back with a curt, "Fuck off," before continuing toward his van.

A mocking remark followed him, "Watch it, he's a Marine." The words hung in the air, a subtle reminder of his past, but John, choosing to let it slide, walked on. Sometimes, the banter on the edge of disrespect was a storm that needed no confrontation. As he approached his van, the comment trailing behind him like a faint echo, John reaffirmed his commitment to rise above the petty squabbles of the sorting office.

The magpies' omen, he thought, held the promise of joy despite the chaos that Wednesday threatened to unleash. With a stoic resolve and the knowledge that even the most turbulent days could be weathered, John set off on his delivery route, determined to turn the day's challenges into triumphs and, perhaps, find joy amid the chaos.

Chapter 19: Echoes of the Night

As dawn painted the cityscape with hues of muted gold, John found himself immersed in the early morning symphony of urban sounds. The rhythmic pulse of the city, amplified by the distant hum of traffic and the occasional screech of tires, wove a tapestry that brought him back to the present. Yet, amid the familiar sounds, one element stood out—a haunting chorus carried by the night air.

Sirens, the nocturnal ballad of emergency response vehicles, echoed through the city. The wailing notes cut through the stillness, each siren telling a story of urgency, of lives hanging in the balance. The distinct tones hinted at the nature of the emergency—Police, fire brigade, or ambulance—racing towards scenes of peril, towards the unknown challenges the night had birthed.

John, standing amidst the awakening city, listened to the sirens with a mix of reflection and gratitude. The night air, heavy with the echoes of emergency calls, stirred memories of those he had lost in the past. Friends and comrades, taken by the unpredictable currents of life. His reflective gaze lingered on the quiet acknowledgment that survival was a gift.

He loved the city—the vibrant tapestry of cultures, the eclectic blend of life—but he knew its dual nature. A place pulsating with energy and danger, where the night's revelry could swiftly transform into moments of chaos and crisis. Stabbings, shootings, accidents fuelled by alcohol and drugs, a city that didn't sleep but sometimes awoke to nightmares.

As he prepared for the day's deliveries, the sounds of sirens served as a reminder of life's fragility. The city, with its heartbeat echoing through the wail of emergency vehicles, was a living entity with its own ebb and flow of joy and tragedy. The sirens, once ominous, now became a melodic affirmation of life's vitality.

The icy roads of the city, especially in the early hours, bore witness to the aftermath of chaotic nights. Yet, amidst the potential peril, John couldn't deny the thrill he felt as the sirens cut through the air. They were the city's heartbeat, a testament to its resilience and vitality. The city had its perils, but it also possessed a unique pulse that made him feel alive.

With the echoes of sirens fading into the distance, John embraced the day ahead. The streets, still bathed in the early morning glow, awaited his footsteps. As he navigated the city's arteries, he carried with him the knowledge that life, much like the urban symphony, was a delicate balance—a blend of danger and vibrancy that made every moment precious.

Chapter 20: A New Horizon

As John traversed the city streets, he found himself reflecting on a facet of his life that had undergone a seismic shift. For four decades, he had been immersed in environments where skill, expertise, and shared experiences bound individuals together. His time in the Royal Marines and the subsequent three decades offshore on a Diving Support Vessel had cocooned him in a world of like-minded professionals, a tight-knit community of individuals with specialized skills.

Now, in his role as a postman, he was navigating a different landscape—one where normalcy, routine, and the everyday took precedence. The people he interacted with weren't fellow marines or offshore experts; they were the fabric of everyday society. Nine-to-fivers, home keepers diligently saving for that annual two-week holiday with the kids, individuals leading lives that revolved around the ordinary rhythms of everyday existence.

This marked a stark departure from the familiarity of his past. The banter in the sorting office, the conversations on doorsteps, and the snippets of daily life exchanged with people on his route were windows into a world he had never intimately known. As the people of Nottingham engaged in discussions about the weather, family vacations, and the mundane triumphs and tribulations of everyday life, John discovered a new facet of human connection—one anchored in the shared experiences of normalcy.

He observed with curiosity and interest, recognizing the beauty in the simplicity of these interactions. The amalgamation of diverse voices, each telling a story woven from the threads of commonplace joys and challenges, added a new layer to his understanding of social dynamics. The city, once a backdrop to his deliveries, became a vibrant canvas of human stories.

In the unscripted exchanges on doorsteps and in the sorting office, John was learning about the resilience, humour, and dreams of everyday people. The intricacies of their lives, the universality of their concerns, and the genuine warmth with which they welcomed a postman into their routines became sources of both fascination and appreciation.

As he continued his journey through the city, John marvelled at the richness of this newfound social tapestry. The integration into Nottingham's social life, marked by conversations about the ordinary and the extraordinary, was proving to be a rewarding exploration into the heart of humanity. Each doorstep became a portal to stories of resilience, laughter, and the shared human experience—a mosaic of normalcy that was, in its own way, extraordinary.

Chapter 21: Shadows of Retribution

The day unfolded, and with it came the stark realization that, much like PTSD, certain triggers could awaken dormant demons within John. The triggers, however, were not the ghosts of a war-torn past; they were the echoes of disrespect and condescension. The encounters with people who, in their superiority, opened the door to a darker realm within him.

It was a woman on Brairbank Drive who became the unwitting catalyst for the storm brewing within John. Summoning him over with a tone dripping with condescension, she pointed out, "You posted this yesterday, it's not for here. Look, it says Brairbank Walk, which is over there, I think." The intentional emphasis on 'thinks' and the knowing smirk betrayed her deliberate attempt to humiliate.

For the remainder of his walk, John simmered in a silent rage. The perceived disrespect fanned the flames of vengeance within him. As he navigated the streets, the plot for retribution played out in his mind like a relentless movie reel. Thoughts of payback, of teaching her a lesson in humility, consumed his every step.

The scenarios unfolded in his mind, each one darker and more visceral than the last. Physical actions and their consequences, the aftermath, and the meticulous cover-up became the centrepiece of his thoughts. Hours passed, but the desire for retaliation continued to pulse through his veins, a malevolent energy that refused to be quelled.

In the secret recesses of his mind, John concocted a foolproof plan for vengeance. The satisfaction he derived from imagining her downfall, her suffering, became a twisted balm for the wounded pride inflicted upon him. The sheer creativity with which he devised methods of retribution was both disturbing and captivating.

Several hours later, John emerged from the labyrinth of his thoughts with a macabre sense of satisfaction. The revenge, in his mind, was perfect—her suffering guaranteed, his escape foolproof. The intricate details of the plan had etched themselves into his consciousness, a blueprint for the darkness he harboured.

As he continued his rounds, the weight of his sinister thoughts bore down on him. The city streets, once familiar and filled with the ordinary rhythms of life, now harboured shadows of retribution. The woman on Brairbank Drive remained blissfully unaware of the storm brewing in the mind of the postman.

Unbeknownst to her, the seeds of vengeance had taken root, and in the darkness that lurked behind John's stoic exterior, a storm was gathering—a tempest of aggression, retribution, and the haunting echoes of disrespect that threatened to shatter the fragile equilibrium he had built in the world of everyday people.

Chapter 22: The Abyss Beckons

Within the confines of John's troubled mind, the darkness had taken root, and the shadows of retribution manifested in ways that bespoke his military training. The arsenal of techniques learned during his time in the military, where the objective was often to incapacitate or neutralize an opponent, now became the unsettling instruments in the symphony of vengeance playing in his thoughts.

His mind, once disciplined for strategic and defensive purposes, now contorted these skills into a malevolent dance. Holds that could render limbs unusable, pressure points to induce unconsciousness, and the grim expertise in using knives—all were at the forefront of his contemplation. The preference for the knife seemed to add a sinister layer, a macabre flourish to the revenge he was crafting.

John had been taught the art of inflicting pain during unarmed combat, the controlled use of force to gain the upper hand. Now, however, the intent was not merely to subdue an opponent but to enact a visceral form of vengeance. The thought of wielding a knife, of letting red blood gush and spurt under the pressure of his actions, was a calculated method to induce mental anguish before the final descent into unconsciousness.

In his mental labyrinth, he visualized the scenes—each cut, each crimson spray, a gruesome punctuation in the narrative of his retribution. The psychological torment inflicted by the sight of one's own blood, a prelude to the physical pain that would follow, became a canvas on which he painted the disturbing tableau of his revenge.

The question lingered: how had a moment of perceived disrespect led him down this dark path? The woman on Brairbank Drive, ignorant of the tempest brewing within the postman, continued her daily life, oblivious to the malevolent designs taking shape in the recesses of his consciousness.

As John continued his route, the shadows deepened. The ordinary streets of Nottingham, bathed in the glow of everyday life, now harboured the echoes of a mind on the brink. The abyss beckoned, and the postman, once a harbinger of connection and routine, had become entangled in the snare of his own unravelling psyche.

Whether the revenge would remain a dark fantasy or materialize into a nightmarish reality remained uncertain. The path he walked, both in the city streets and the corridors of his own thoughts, now led him toward an abyss where the boundary between imagination and action blurred—an abyss where the spectre of violence and vengeance held sway over the fragile equilibrium he had sought to maintain.

Chapter 23: Echoes of Murakami

In the quiet solitude of his room, John found himself absorbed in the entrancing world of Haruki Murakami. The pages of "The Wind-Up Bird Chronicle" held Lieutenant Mamiya's tale, a narrative etched with haunting brutality, vivid details, and an emotional intensity that lingered in the air like an indelible echo. The scene was a masterful stroke, painting a canvas of raw humanity against the backdrop of Murakami's unique blend of magical realism.

As he continued his literary exploration, another door opened, leading him into the surreal corridors of "Kafka on the Shore." Here, Murakami wove a narrative tapestry where Kafka, amidst dreamlike sequences blending reality and fantasy, confronted an intense event involving his father. It was a moment charged with an emotional intensity that cut through the pages and settled in the reader's soul, leaving an impression that transcended mere storytelling.

Yet, within the tapestry of Murakami's words, John recognized the subjective nature of disturbance. What stirred the depths of his emotions might not evoke the same response in another. The novelist's ability to delve into complex human experiences, even when faced with challenging or unconventional themes, became a testament to the power of literature to resonate on a deeply personal level.

In this contemplative moment, John realized the profound impact of Murakami's work. It was a mirror reflecting the myriad facets of human emotion, a journey through surreal landscapes and intense emotional landscapes that left an indelible mark on the reader's psyche. As he considered the scenes that others might find disturbing, he marvelled at the transformative power of literature to illuminate the hidden recesses of the human experience.

Different readers, like voyagers through the pages of Murakami's novels, embarked on unique journeys, each resonating with distinct scenes based on their own perspectives and experiences. In this quiet room, surrounded by the echoes of Murakami's narratives, John understood the profound truth that literature, at its core, is a deeply personal and subjective exploration of the human soul.

Chapter 24: Shadows of Discomfort

As John navigated the familiar terrain of Brairbank Avenue, a peculiar shadow trailed him—a phantom born from the depths of his contemplations. The weight of Lieutenant Mamiya's harrowing tale, as spun by the masterful wordsmith Haruki Murakami, lingered like an unwelcome spectre in the recesses of his thoughts.

The houses along the avenue, once mere structures in a routine delivery route, now seemed to whisper echoes of discomfort. Each mailbox, each doorbell, became a conduit for the haunting images of the Japanese spy subjected to the cruelties of his captors. John, usually immersed in the daily choreography of parcel deliveries, found his mind entangled in the threads of Murakami's narrative.

The letters and packages in his hands, while tangible and ordinary, assumed a weight of symbolism. Each doorstep he approached carried a subtle reminder of the frailty of the human experience, an undercurrent of vulnerability echoing through the mundane act of delivering mail. The comfort of routine now mingled with the discomfort of empathizing with a character ensnared in the clutches of despair.

As the day unfolded, the book's chapter became an indomitable companion, walking alongside him in the form of spectral discomfort. The corners of Brairbank Avenue, once familiar and unassuming, now harboured shadows that danced with the lingering imagery of Lieutenant Mamiya's tribulations.

The juxtaposition of the ordinary and the extraordinary heightened the poignancy of each doorstep encounter. In this ordinary suburban landscape, the extraordinary lingered in the unspoken words between neighbours, in the rustle of leaves on the pavement, and in the quietude that enveloped the street.

As he pressed on with his deliveries, John wrestled with the interplay of reality and fiction. The discomfort seeded by Murakami's words had taken root, transforming the routine into a contemplative journey through the nuances of human suffering and resilience. And so, with each letter delivered and each step taken along Brairbank Avenue, the echoes of that haunting chapter continued to shape the contours of John's introspection.

Chapter 25: A Subtle Symphony of Revenge

As the echoes of Lieutenant Mamiya's tale continued to reverberate in John's mind, so did the unsettling discomfort caused by the woman's condescending tone. The ordinary act of delivering mail transformed into a stage for a quiet, calculated symphony of revenge. John, spurred by wounded pride and a desire to reclaim his dignity, formulated a plan that unfolded like a subtle and deliberate overture.

Every step along the familiar paths of St. Annes bore witness to the orchestration of his reprisal. Instead of overt hostility, John opted for a more nuanced approach—a delicate dance of psychological retaliation. Armed with a well-crafted strategy, he executed his plan with precision, covering all his bases like a conductor guiding each instrument in a symphony.

The first note of his revenge symphony played out in casual conversations with other residents, strategically dropping hints and carefully constructed anecdotes that subtly shifted perceptions. The composition continued with gestures of generosity, earning him the favour and sympathy of those who had once witnessed the lady's disdain.

With each passing house, he planted seeds of doubt and curiosity, encouraging neighbours to question the authenticity of the lady's actions. The web of whispers and subtle insinuations grew, creating a delicate tapestry of doubt that wrapped around her reputation like a silken thread.

The crescendo of John's revenge unfolded as he strategically timed his encounters with the lady, engaging her in seemingly innocuous conversations that subtly probed her vulnerabilities. He exploited the art of subtlety, leaving her disarmed and exposed, uncertain of the currents swirling beneath the surface.

As his revenge symphony reached its finale, the lady, unaware of the subtle manipulations at play, found herself isolated within the harmonious community she had once considered her own. The balance of power shifted quietly, leaving John with a sense of vindication, a silent victory that resonated more profoundly than any overt confrontation.

In the end, St. Annes remained a stage for the quiet drama of human interactions, each resident playing their part in the intricate dance of community life. John, having orchestrated his revenge with finesse, continued his rounds with a newfound sense of dignity, the echoes of Lieutenant Mamiya's story fading into the background as the curtain fell on this chapter of his life.

Chapter 26: Reflections and Realizations

Amidst the orchestrated ballet of subtle revenge and the ebb and flow of St. Annes' daily life, John found himself at a crossroads, contemplating not only his past but also the path that stretched ahead. The rhythm of his footsteps on the uneven pavements echoed the cadence of his thoughts, a melodic reflection on the state of the Royal Mail and his role within it.

The privatization of the postal service in 2013 had cast a looming shadow over the institution, altering its dynamics and, in John's eyes, diminishing the once-pristine reputation of the post office. The influx of packet deliveries, a consequence of the changing landscape, left the posties overburdened, racing against the clock to fulfil their duties, leaving little room for the genuine interactions that once defined the service.

As the days shortened and the nights drew in, John felt the strain of the overloaded rounds. The charm of quick exchanges with bored housewives, once a fleeting respite, now became a bittersweet reminder of the constraints imposed by time and the mounting pressures on postal services.

Reflecting on these challenges, John wrestled with the realization that the very essence of the Royal Mail, a service built on community engagement and personal connections, was gradually eroding. The disenchanted homeowners and their lack of respect seemed symptomatic of a larger issue—the widening gap between the public and the institution meant to serve them.

In this moment of contemplation, John envisioned a future where the Royal Mail could reclaim its former glory, a future where community connections were prioritized over parcel volumes. A sense of responsibility stirred within him, a desire to be a catalyst for change, to bridge the gap that had widened over the years.

As the postal service navigated the challenges of modernization, John pondered how he could contribute to restoring its former sense of pride. Perhaps it was time to advocate for a return to the fundamentals of genuine service, to address the imbalance and ensure that the posties had the time and support they needed to engage meaningfully with the public.

The future, uncertain yet rife with possibilities, awaited John's decisions. With each step, he considered how he could be a beacon of change within the Royal Mail, a force to rekindle the fading flame of community and connection.

Chapter 27: Unintended Allies

In a moment of vulnerability, John found himself confiding in a man whose interests seemed to align with his own frustrations and grievances. The man, intrigued by John's plot to retaliate against the disrespectful homeowner, became an unintentional ally, his curiosity transforming into an eerie enthusiasm for the vengeful plan.

As John unfolded the details of his scheme, he expected a fellow disgruntled soul, perhaps a sympathetic nod or a shared understanding of the frustration that had fueled his desire for revenge. However, the man's response took an unexpected turn. Instead of expressing empathy, he delved into intricate suggestions on how to execute the plan with precision, weaving a web of meticulous details aimed at covering John's actions.

The man's guidance, while extensive and seemingly well-intentioned, sent a chill down John's spine. The level of expertise and insight into evading the authorities far exceeded what John had anticipated. His initial sense of relief at finding a sympathetic ear twisted into a knot of unease.

A realization dawned on John that he had inadvertently involved someone who wasn't merely a passive listener but rather an active participant in the dark depths of his plan. The advice offered went beyond a mere exchange of grievances; it was a roadmap for someone well-versed in concealing illicit activities.

As he listened to the man's detailed instructions, John couldn't shake the feeling that he had crossed a dangerous threshold. The intricate web of suggestions painted a picture of a sinister alliance, raising questions about the man's motivations and expertise in matters best left unexplored.

With a growing sense of discomfort, John understood the gravity of his mistake. There was no room for error, in this endeavour; it was meant to be a solitary act of retribution, a personal catharsis. The unintended ally's enthusiasm for covering tracks hinted at a darker agenda, and John found himself questioning the consequences of sharing his plan with this stranger.

As the echoes of the man's suggestions lingered, John grappled with the realization that he had unknowingly invited a complicating factor into his solitary pursuit of justice. The journey ahead seemed fraught with uncertainty, and the unintended alliance cast a shadow over the revenge he had initially sought.

Chapter 28: A Hazy Morning of Reflection

The morning after confiding in the unintended ally left John with a throbbing headache and a gnawing sense of regret. The cozy ambiance of the Whistle and Flute, with its warm lights and friendly chatter, had been overshadowed by the unintended consequences of sharing his revenge plot. As he groaned through the hangover, he realized the weight of the secret he had let slip.

Regret settled over him like a heavy fog, obscuring the clarity of his initial intentions. The desire for retribution, once burning bright, now felt clouded by the unforeseen alliance forged in the dimly lit corners of the pub. The hangover served as a tangible reminder of the blurred lines between confiding and colluding.

In the cold light of day, John questioned whether the path he had set foot upon was one he truly wanted to tread. The fervour for revenge had dissipated, replaced by a sobering sense of responsibility for the potential consequences of his actions. The unintended ally's suggestions lingered in his mind, a haunting reminder of the dark avenues that revenge could lead down.

With a heavy heart, John resolved to abandon the quest for retribution. The burden of the plan and the unintended alliance had dampened the holiday spirit that surrounded him. The Royal Mail's parcels, now laden with the joy and anticipation of Christmas, seemed to mock the darker motivations that had driven him.

As he navigated the streets overloaded with emotions and parcels, John contemplated the weight of forgiveness. The Christmas presents, entrusted to him by the Royal Mail, held the hopes and dreams of the senders and receivers. It was a reminder that amidst the tumult of personal grievances, there existed a shared humanity that transcended revenge.

The romantic trysts he had envisioned during his rounds seemed a distant fantasy, overshadowed by the complexity of human emotions and the need for genuine connections. During the holiday hustle, John found solace in the idea of letting go, in forgiving and moving forward.

As the day unfolded, he embraced the busy chaos of the season, immersing himself in the task at hand. The Christmas presents, symbols of joy and goodwill, became a catalyst for a shift in perspective. John, burdened by regret, chose to forge a different path—one illuminated by the spirit of forgiveness and the promise of a brighter, more compassionate future.

Chapter 29: Reflections on Wheels

In a spur of creativity and a desire to capture the essence of his unique journey, John set up his iPhone inside the van before embarking on his daily rounds through Saint Anns. The small device became a witness to his musings and contemplations as he drove, a confessional on wheels capturing the raw, unfiltered essence of his experiences.

Throughout the day, John would record short snippets—20 to 30 seconds each—sharing his inner thoughts, observations, and the occasional anecdote. The van, once a vessel for parcels and letters, transformed into a mobile stage for John's reflections, a rolling diary that chronicled the trials and tribulations of a postman navigating the streets of Saint Anns.

As he drove through the familiar lanes and alleys, John's commentary offered a glimpse into the multifaceted nature of his world. He spoke of the challenges of the job, the peculiarities of the residents, and the nuances of each neighbourhood. The mundane moments became infused with a sense of significance, and the ordinary transformed into something worth documenting.

When the day's rounds were complete and John returned home that night, he played back the collection of clips. The audio snapshots revealed the spectrum of emotions, from frustration to joy, and the subtle beauty hidden within the routine of delivering mail. Watching the snippets in succession, John realized that he had inadvertently created a narrative—a personal chronicle of his time as a postie.

Inspired by the recordings, John entertained the idea of crafting a short movie encapsulating the essence of his experiences. The prospect of sharing his unique perspective on the world of postal delivery intrigued him. The snippets, like confessions from the road, became the building blocks for a visual story that could offer a glimpse into the life of a postman navigating the streets of Saint Anns.

The notion of transforming his daily routine into a cinematic venture brought a renewed sense of purpose and creativity. As he considered the potential audience for his short movie, John envisioned not just a documentation of his journey but a celebration of the ordinary, a tribute to the unsung heroes driving the wheels of the Royal Mail through the heart of the community.

With newfound enthusiasm, John embarked on the next phase of his project—shaping the recorded confessions into a cohesive narrative that would unveil the untold stories of Saint Anns and the man behind the wheel of the postman's van.

Chapter 30: A Question of Motivation

As John delved deeper into his project of recording snippets during his postal rounds, a nagging question surfaced in his mind. Was this endeavour an act of narcissism, a self-indulgent display of his own experiences, or something more profound—a recorded confession intended to leave a mark on the world, a testament to the why behind the seemingly ordinary?

In moments of introspection, he pondered whether the motivation behind this visual diary was purely egocentric or if there was a deeper, more altruistic purpose hidden beneath the surface. Did he embark on this journey of self-documentation to satisfy a personal need for validation, or was it an earnest attempt to offer a glimpse into the life of a postman in Saint Anns?

As the recordings accumulated, the dichotomy of his motivation played out in his mind. On one hand, he acknowledged the inherently personal nature of the project. The snippets captured his thoughts, frustrations, and joys, providing a window into his unique perspective. But on the other hand, he couldn't shake the sense that this could be more than a mere exercise in self-reflection.

Perhaps, he thought, it was his way of communicating with a future audience, a silent plea for understanding and empathy. A recorded confession, not for the sake of personal glorification, but as a testament to the struggles and triumphs of an individual navigating the complexities of life, both as a postman and as a person.

In contemplating the potential future discovery of these recordings, John wondered if he was leaving behind a legacy or a puzzle for those who would come after him. Was it a deliberate act of self-expression or an inadvertent cry for connection across time?

As he continued to record his thoughts and experiences, the question of motivation lingered. Was it driven by narcissism, a desire for recognition, or was it an attempt to bridge the gap between the ordinary and the extraordinary, to showcase the humanity behind the mundane?

The uncertainty added a layer of complexity to his project, turning each recorded snippet into a multifaceted reflection of his intentions. As the van traversed the familiar streets of Saint Anns, John grappled with the enigma of his own motivations, unsure whether he was the protagonist or a mere spectator in the unfolding narrative of his recorded confessions.

Chapter 31: Reconnections and Perspectives

In an unexpected turn of events, John found himself reconnected with an old friend from his past, Debby. Their shared history traced back to their school days in the '70s, and now, after over 40 years, life had brought them together again. Debby, who had transitioned from being a postie to driving buses in Nottingham, reached out to John, sparking a reunion that carried the weight of decades of untold stories.

As they reminisced about their youth and caught up on the years that had passed, Debby expressed disbelief upon learning about John's current role as a postman. The coincidence of their paths crossing twice in one day along Derby Road seemed almost serendipitous, creating a sense of wonder at the twists and turns life could take.

Debby, now a bus driver, shared insights from her own career transition. She emphasized the sentiment that being a postie was the best job in the world. Her words hung in the air, echoing a perspective shaped by years of experience on both sides of the Royal Mail's operations.

However, John, still grappling with his evolving perception of the job, remained sceptical. His recent experiences, entangled with moments of frustration and reflections on respect, cast shadows on the romanticized notion of the perfect postman's job. The clash with disrespectful homeowners and the unanticipated challenges had stirred a complexity that lingered in his thoughts.

As they walked together along Derby Road, dogs at their side, John couldn't help but marvel at the twists of fate that had brought them back into each other's lives. Debby's conviction about the virtues of being a postie lingered in his mind, challenging his doubts, and inviting him to reconsider the potential joys of the job.

The reunion with Debby not only revived old connections but also planted seeds of contemplation in John's evolving narrative. Would the shared experiences of former colleagues shed light on the aspects of the job that he had yet to fully appreciate? The answer, perhaps, lay in the unfolding chapters of his journey as a postman in Saint Anns.

Chapter 32: Unforeseen Interrogations

The atmosphere in the manager's office took an unexpected turn as Luke ushered John in to meet two stern-faced men. A glance at their demeanour instantly triggered a recognition in John—he knew that stance, that air of authority. The two men were detectives from Central, and a chill ran down John's spine.

Luke, with a solemn expression, introduced the detectives, making it clear that this encounter was more than routine. John, while trying to maintain composure, couldn't help but feel a sense of unease settling in the room.

As the detectives began their questioning, John's mind raced to revisit the recent events. He had believed he covered his tracks meticulously after the incident he referred to as "the flaying." Confidence in his ability to navigate through routine police inquiries began to waver as the questions took on a more probing nature.

The detectives delved into details, dissecting the events surrounding the incident in question. John's attempts to provide clear and concise answers were met with scrutinizing gazes, indicating that this was anything but a routine inquiry.

Despite his initial confidence, doubts crept in. Had he overlooked a crucial detail? Was there a loose end he failed to tie up? The room, once a familiar space within the confines of the sorting office, now felt like an interrogation chamber amplifying the gravity of the situation.

As the questioning continued, John couldn't shake the feeling that the detectives were gradually peeling back layers of his carefully constructed narrative. What had seemed like a controlled situation now hung in the balance, and the presence of law enforcement added a weight to the consequences of his actions.

In the midst of the unfolding interrogation, John grappled with the realization that his assumed mastery of the situation might have been an illusion. The two detectives, unyielding in their pursuit of truth, pushed the boundaries of his explanations, leaving him to navigate a precarious dance between his past actions and the consequences that now loomed before him.

Chapter 33: A Delicate Dance of Questions

The detectives' questions continued, each inquiry like a carefully calculated move in a delicate dance of information. "On the 23rd of November, during your round in Saint Annes, did you deliver mail to Number 11 Brairbank Avenue?" The words hung in the air, and John's response was swift and confident, a product of his military background. "No, Sir."

His disciplined manner conveyed a sense of control, a demeanour shaped by years of military service. Yet, beneath the surface, a subtle tension lingered. As he recalled that particular morning, a mental slideshow played images of houses, doorsteps, and faces.

The detectives, adept at reading subtle cues, probed further. Unbeknownst to John, the intricate web of interactions on that fateful day was under scrutiny. Did anyone witness his movements from one house to the next? Was there an inadvertent observer who could potentially unravel the carefully woven fabric of his alibi?

The dance of questions continued, each step revealing more about the intricacies of that November morning. The detectives, like skilled partners in a dance, led John through a series of inquiries, probing for inconsistencies or hidden nuances in his narrative.

For a moment, the manager's office transformed into an arena where the past and present collided. John, accustomed to facing challenges head-on, maintained his stoic facade. Yet, beneath the surface, a subtle undercurrent of uncertainty flowed. Had he overlooked a crucial detail? Would the detectives uncover a chink in the armour of his carefully constructed story?

As the questioning persisted, John couldn't help but wonder about the chain of events set in motion. The routine queries, seemingly innocuous, formed the threads of a narrative that could sway the balance between truth and fiction.

In the hushed confines of the manager's office, the detectives guided the conversation, unravelling the layers of that pivotal day. With each question, the delicate dance continued, leaving John to navigate the intricate steps between his recollections and the unseen eyes that sought to unveil the truth.

Chapter 34: The Interrogation Room Revelations

The dimly lit interrogation room at the central station set the stage for a pivotal moment in John's unfolding story. The detectives, faces partially shadowed by the harsh lighting, scrutinized the footage captured by the doorbell devices at Numbers 15 and 11 Brairbank Avenue. The flickering screen displayed moments frozen in time, a silent witness to the interactions that transpired on that crucial day.

Detective Mitchell, a stern figure with a penetrating gaze, leaned forward. "Mr. MacGregor, the footage clearly shows you interacting with the woman at Number 11 on the 23rd of November. Care to explain why you stated otherwise?"

John, facing the detectives across the table, maintained his composure. "Sir, I apologize for any confusion. My initial response was based on my recollection of that day. It appears I misspoke."

Detective Parker, a seasoned investigator, chimed in. "Misspoke or not, we need the truth, Mr. MacGregor. Now, can you tell us about the events leading up to and following that interaction at Number 11?"

John, recalibrating his thoughts, began to recount the sequence of events. "On the 23rd, I delivered mail to Number 15, and the woman there called me over. As for Number 11, I interacted briefly, exchanged pleasantries, and went on with my round."

Detective Mitchell, pointing at the screen, pressed on. "Two days later, on the 25th, you revisited Number 11. Why?"

John, aware of the significance of this moment, chose his words carefully. "Sir, it was a routine delivery. I followed my usual route, and it happened to include Number 11."

Detective Parker, scrutinizing the footage, remarked, "Routine or not, Mr. MacGregor, the frequency of your visits to Number 11 raises questions. Can you explain why you went back so soon?"

John, maintaining his stoic demeanour, responded, "Sir, it's not uncommon for residents to receive multiple deliveries during the holiday season. I was merely fulfilling my duty."

The detectives, unsatisfied but lacking concrete evidence, continued their line of questioning. The exchange between them and John unfolded like a verbal chess match, each move calculated and measured. In the muted ambiance of the interrogation room, the truth hung in the balance, waiting to reveal itself amidst the questions and answers that danced on the precipice of revelation.

Chapter 35: Unravelling Threads

The forensics team, armed with a search warrant and a meticulous approach, descended upon John's residence. Their mission: to unravel the threads that could potentially connect him to the mysterious and disturbing incident involving the woman at Number 11.

As the investigators donned their protective gear, a symphony of activity unfolded within the confines of John's home. The search for clues began in earnest, each member of the team assigned to a specific area, methodically examining the surroundings for any trace that might link John to the alleged crime.

DNA Collection: The forensics team focused on collecting DNA samples from various surfaces, carefully swabbing areas that might harbour microscopic evidence. They targeted items frequently touched or used by John, seeking to establish a forensic link between him and the woman at Number 11.

Fiber Analysis: A meticulous examination of clothing, carpets, and personal belongings ensued. The team meticulously catalogued and analysed any fibres found, looking for matches that could provide a tangible connection between John and the crime scene.

Footprint and Shoe Print Comparison: The investigators paid close attention to footwear impressions, both within the house and in areas of potential interest. Comparisons were drawn between the patterns and sizes of John's shoes and any imprints discovered during the forensic examination.

Documented Possessions: Personal items, such as clothing and accessories, underwent scrutiny. The forensics team documented and analysed each possession, searching for any anomalies or traces that might tie John to the events of that fateful day.

Surveillance Footage: Beyond the physical realm, the team sought access to any surveillance footage from nearby cameras that might capture John's movements on the days in question. The digital trail could serve as a vital piece in reconstructing the timeline of events.

The search unfolded like a puzzle, with each collected piece offering a potential glimpse into the truth. The forensics team, guided by the gravity of their task, navigated through the labyrinth of John's life, seeking to uncover any hidden connection that could explain the disturbing events surrounding Number 11.

As the forensic investigation progressed, the weight of uncertainty hung in the air. In this intricate dance of science and scrutiny, the truth lay concealed, waiting to be unearthed from the carefully examined fragments of John's world.

Chapter 37: The Vanishing Illusion

The forensics team, in their relentless pursuit of truth, stumbled upon a crucial piece of the puzzle. Hidden within the folds of John MacGregor's post bag, a revelation lay dormant — evidence linking him to the woman at Number 11. The discovery sent shockwaves through the investigation, shattering the illusion of an airtight alibi.

Unbeknownst to John, the post bag he believed securely stowed in his van harbored a secret. Forensic experts, armed with the authority granted by the ongoing investigation, gained access to the vehicle, a move that caught John off guard. Traces of the woman's DNA found on the post bag became the linchpin that threatened to unravel the carefully constructed facade of innocence.

Armed with this newfound evidence, the authorities concluded that they had enough grounds to make an arrest. The looming spectre of legal action cast a shadow over John's routine, and the once-sturdy walls he had built around himself began to crumble. His understanding of the military interrogation process didn't fully prepare him for the complexities of civilian legal proceedings.

As the first brick fell, John pondered the fragility of the towering structure he had erected in his life. The stability he once took for granted now faced the unsettling prospect of collapse. The domino effect of legal proceedings seemed inevitable, and the gravity of the situation weighed heavily on him.

However, John MacGregor, a veteran of military discipline and resilience, did not crumble under the pressure. He drew upon the strength forged in the crucible of his past experiences. The looming arrest, the potential trial, and the scrutiny of his personal life were hurdles he approached with a stoic resolve.

As the legal machinery commenced its inexorable march, John braced himself for the intricate dance of legal proceedings. The familiar dance of 'good cop,' 'bad cop' played out anew, dredging up his past, his failed marriages, and his struggle to find his place in civilian society.

In this chapter of uncertainty, John MacGregor faced a formidable adversary — not on the battlefield, but within the intricate web of the justice system. The illusion of invincibility shattered, leaving him to navigate the complexities of a legal landscape where the past and present converged, threatening to rewrite the narrative of his life.

Chapter 38: Shadows of Accusation

As news of John MacGregor's arrest spread through the hallowed halls of the delivery office, a murmur of shock and disbelief rippled among his colleagues. The man who had walked the familiar paths of Saint Anns, delivering mail with a gruff demeanour and a repertoire of dark humour, now found himself at the centre of a heinous accusation. The details of the alleged crime were embellished with each retelling, taking on a life of their own within the echoing walls of the sorting office.

The older hands, who had always harboured a suspicion about John's peculiarities, exchanged uneasy glances. How could someone they interacted with daily, someone they shared jokes and banter within the pre-dawn hours, be capable of such a monstrous act? The graphic details, fuelled by speculation and imagination, seeped into every conversation, creating an atmosphere thick with judgment and uncertainty.

Meanwhile, behind the cold bars of a jail cell, John contemplated his defence strategy. The police had only a shred of evidence, and he clung to the belief that a skilled solicitor could dismantle their case. As he prepared for the impending trial, the prospect of pleading 'Not guilty' loomed large. His defence would need to be meticulous, exploiting the weaknesses in the prosecution's case while shielding him from the shadows of accusation.

The day of the initial consultation with his lawyer arrived. Seated in the stark confines of the prison's interview room, John met his legal representative, a beacon of hope in his tumultuous journey through the legal system.

Lawyer: Mr. MacGregor, thank you for meeting with me. Let us delve into the details of your case. The police have a thin strand of evidence, but we must ensure it does not turn into a noose.

John: (Nodding) I've maintained my innocence from the start. They do not have anything concrete.

Lawyer: Excellent. We will challenge the veracity of their evidence and emphasize any procedural lapses. We need to create reasonable doubt in the minds of the jury.

John: What about the coroner's report that got leaked? It's making me look like a monster.

Lawyer: We will address that too. We will argue that the leak compromised the presumption of innocence and tainted public opinion. Our focus will be on the legal facts, not sensationalized narratives.

The lawyer, with a strategic mind and unwavering confidence, outlined a plan to navigate the upcoming trial. As they discussed tactics and scenarios, John found a glimmer of hope amid the gloom of his incarceration. The courtroom, he realized, would become the arena where truth clashed with perception, and his defence would be the shield against the shadows of accusation.

In this chapter of uncertainty, the legal battle loomed on the horizon, and John MacGregor braced himself for a fight that would determine not only his freedom but also the restoration of his tarnished reputation.

Chapter 39: Reflections Behind Bars

The cold, unforgiving walls of the jail cell echoed with the sounds of solitude. John MacGregor found himself confined once again, not in the disciplined confines of a military detention centre, but within the stark reality of a civilian prison. As he sat on the narrow bed, memories from almost four decades ago resurfaced, reminiscent of the days spent in 'Pompy DQ's,' the Royal Navy/Royal Marines detention centre in Portsmouth.

He recalled the rigid routines, the hard bunk beds, and the incessant drills that punctuated his time in military custody. Yet, here he was, questioning his existence behind bars once more. The floor, his makeshift bed, became a sanctuary for sleep, ensuring his actual bed and bedding were impeccably maintained for morning inspections. Those experiences seemed like echoes from a bygone era, an era now juxtaposed with the harsh reality of present circumstances.

"Why am I locked up like an animal?" he wondered, the question reverberating through the confines of his thoughts. In his mind, the incident that led to his incarceration bore a twisted sense of justice—a means to rid society of a condescending and disrespectful member. Wasn't he, in a way, serving a purpose?

Amid the solitude, a knock on the cell door signalled the intrusion of the prison psychiatrist. The probing questions about his childhood, his military life, and the incident that led him to this juncture sought to construct a psychological profile. John, guarded but introspective, navigated the inquiries, each answer revealing layers of a complex persona shaped by years of military discipline and a growing disdain for disrespect.

Psychiatrist: Mr. MacGregor, let's delve into your past. How would you describe your childhood?

John: (Reflecting) It was tough, but it prepared me for the challenges ahead. Discipline was ingrained early on.

Psychiatrist: And your time in the military? How did that shape your outlook on authority and discipline?

John: (Pausing) The military taught me the value of order and respect. It instilled a sense of duty. But, it also showed me the darker side of power dynamics.

As the interview continued, the psychiatrist probed deeper into the nuances of John's psyche. The juxtaposition of military order and civilian chaos, of duty and disdain, painted a multifaceted portrait. Behind the hardened exterior lay a man grappling with conflicting notions of justice and societal expectations.

As the session concluded, John returned to the solitude of his cell, where the echoes of his past mingled with the uncertainty of the present. The psychological evaluation, a mere snapshot of his intricate life, added another layer to the complex narrative unfolding within the confines of the prison walls.

Chapter 40: Crafting a Defence

With the trial looming on the horizon, John MacGregor's defence team gathered in a dimly lit conference room to strategize. The air was thick with tension as the lawyers exchanged glances, each one burdened with the weight of the impending legal battle. Around a cluttered table strewn with case files, they began to craft a defence that would challenge the prosecution's narrative.

defence Attorney 1: Alright, let's review the evidence we have and identify the weaknesses in the prosecution's case.

defence Attorney 2: (Flipping through documents) The forensic evidence ties him to the scene, but it doesn't establish intent. We need to exploit that.

defence Attorney 3: (Nodding) Agreed. Our angle should focus on the absence of clear motive. Without a motive, the case weakens.

Lead defence Attorney: (Tapping a pen thoughtfully) And we can't overlook his military background. Let's use that to our advantage. Portray him as a disciplined individual who, under extreme circumstances, took what he believed was a justified action.

The defence team delved into a detailed analysis of every piece of evidence, scrutinizing it from various angles. The absence of a clear motive became a pivotal point of discussion, and they strategized on how to exploit this weakness in the prosecution's case.

defence Attorney 1: (Looking at the timeline) We also have an alibi for the critical timeframe. Witnesses who can vouch for his whereabouts.

defence Attorney 2: (Smirking) That puts a dent in the prosecution's timeline. If he wasn't there when they claim he was, their entire narrative unravels.

Lead defence Attorney: (Leaning back) Excellent. Let's use that to create reasonable doubt. We'll argue that the evidence doesn't conclusively link him to the crime.

As the defence team continued to brainstorm, they shaped a narrative that played to John's strengths – his military background, discipline, and the absence of a clear motive. The alibi provided a solid foundation for introducing doubt into the prosecution's version of events.

Lead defence Attorney: (Addressing the team) We'll build a case that questions the prosecution's key assertions. If we can create reasonable doubt, the jury may not convict.

The room fell into a determined silence as the defence team committed to their strategy. The trial awaited, a battlefield where narratives clashed, and the outcome hinged on the persuasive power of words and evidence. The plan was set, but the real test lay in how well they could navigate the intricate dance of legal arguments in the courtroom.

Chapter 41: The Graphic Account

In the confines of his prison cell, John MacGregor felt an urgent need to document the events of that fateful morning with excruciating detail. He sat at a small, rickety desk, the dim light casting shadows across the cramped space. Armed with a pen and a pad of paper, he began to chronicle the disturbing sequence of actions that had led him to this point.

The scratching of the pen against the paper echoed in the silence of the cell as John delved into the darkest recesses of his memory. His vivid recollections flowed onto the pages, a graphic and unfiltered account of the morning in question. Every detail, every nuance, was laid bare – a raw and unapologetic narrative that left nothing to the imagination.

As he wrote, he could almost feel the weight of each word. The ink on the paper became a conduit for the intensity of his emotions, the pen an extension of his troubled psyche. The act of detailing the events seemed to be both a cathartic release and a methodical preparation for what lay ahead.

The Defence team, when presented with this visceral account, was taken aback. The explicit nature of the writing left an uncomfortable atmosphere in the room. They questioned John's motives – why would he provide such a graphic recollection of the incident?

Lead Defence Attorney: (Frowning) This is... detailed, to say the least. Why lay it all out like this?

John MacGregor: (Looking straight ahead) They need to understand. The jury, everyone. They need to see it how I saw it.

Defence Attorney 1: (Exchanging glances) But, John, this level of detail...

John MacGregor: (Interrupting) There's no room for ambiguity. I want them to know the truth, even if it's uncomfortable.

The Defence team, grappling with the unexpected nature of John's account, realized that he was determined to confront the reality of his actions head-on. The graphic nature of his narrative, unsettling as it was, seemed to be an attempt to ensure that there was no room for misinterpretation in the courtroom.

Lead Defence Attorney: (Sighing) We'll need to approach this strategically during the trial. Make sure the jury sees it as a desperate act in extreme circumstances.

As the trial approached, the Defence team faced the challenge of presenting John's narrative in a way that conveyed the complexities of his state of mind without alienating the jury. The unsettling account would become a pivotal element in shaping the Defence strategy, navigating the thin line between understanding and condemnation.

Chapter 42: The Battle for Sanity

In the dimly lit courtroom, the air was thick with tension as John MacGregor's Defence team prepared to make their case. The prosecution argued that his brutal actions were premeditated, a vengeful act that warranted a murder charge. The Defence, however, had a different strategy – to establish that John was not criminally responsible due to a temporary bout of insanity.

Lead Defence Attorney: (Addressing the jury) Ladies and gentlemen, today, you will hear a narrative that is both troubling and complex. We do not deny the events that transpired on that morning, but we ask you to consider the state of mind of the accused.

The Defence began by presenting John's extensive military history, emphasizing the toll it had taken on his mental health. They brought in expert witnesses, including psychiatrists and psychologists, to testify about the psychological impact of John's past experiences – from his time in the Falklands War to his struggles with post-traumatic stress disorder (PTSD).

Psychiatrist: (Testifying) Mr. MacGregor exhibits clear signs of acute stress disorder and PTSD. The events of his past have left an indelible mark on his mental state.

The Defence meticulously outlined the lead-up to the incident, highlighting the series of triggers that culminated in John's extreme response. They delved into his struggle to adapt to civilian life, the daily challenges he faced as a postman, and the constant reminders of his traumatic past.

Defence Attorney 2: (Addressing the jury) In his mind, he believed this drastic action was the only way to confront the disrespect and perceived threats he faced. It was a desperate act, born out of a distorted sense of reality.

The Defence argued that, in the moment, John's perception of the situation had been severely warped by the ghosts of his past. They presented the graphic account, not as a calculated confession, but as a manifestation of his mental state at the time.

Lead Defence Attorney: (Concluding) We are not asking you to condone his actions, but we urge you to consider whether a man so haunted by his past can truly be held criminally responsible.

As the trial unfolded, the battle for John's sanity became a central theme. The jury faced the challenging task of navigating the fine line between accountability and understanding. The best-case scenario for John hinged on convincing the court that, in the throes of his mental struggles, he had lost control, paving the way for a verdict of not guilty by reason of insanity.

The courtroom drama unfolded, leaving the fate of John MacGregor hanging in the balance – a precarious dance between justice and mercy.

Chapter 43: A Shocking Revelation

As the trial progressed, the courtroom was filled with a palpable sense of anticipation. The prosecution, aiming to drive home the brutality of John's actions, chose a dramatic moment to introduce photographic evidence. The images flickered onto the screen, casting an eerie glow over the hushed audience.

Gasps and audible sobs resonated through the courtroom as the vivid and graphic images filled the visual field. Spectators, including John's former postal colleagues, recoiled in horror. The stark reality of the crime he was accused of hit them like a tidal wave. Many couldn't reconcile the person they knew as John MacGregor with the ghastly scenes unfolding before them.

In the gallery, Jenna and Sarah, two of John's former postal colleagues, exchanged stunned glances. The man they once shared a workplace with, cracked jokes alongside during breaks, and knew as an ordinary postman, now appeared as a perpetrator of unspeakable violence. Some shook their heads in disbelief, unwilling to accept the connection between their former colleague and the horrific images on display.

Jenna: (Whispering) This can't be him. I mean, sure, he was grumpy sometimes, but this... It's beyond belief.

Sarah: (Staring at the images) I never thought he had it in him. I mean, we all had our issues with the job, but this?

The shock and disbelief rippled through the courtroom, creating an unsettling atmosphere. The Defence team, keenly aware of the impact of these visuals on the jury and spectators alike, faced the daunting challenge of redirecting the narrative. They needed to shift the focus back to John's mental state and away from the graphic images that had cast a dark shadow over the proceedings.

Lead Defence Attorney: (Addressing the jury) What you've witnessed is undoubtedly disturbing. However, we implore you to look beyond the shocking images and consider the tormented state of mind our client was in.

The Defence worked tirelessly to reframe the narrative, steering the focus back towards the psychological factors that might have contributed to John's actions. The challenge was immense, and the courtroom remained a battlefield of emotions, torn between the visceral impact of the photographs and the intricate arguments of the Defence.

As the trial continued, the jurors, faced the unenviable task of balancing their emotional responses to the shocking evidence with the legal responsibility of impartial judgment. The question lingered in the air – could they find compassion for a man whose past haunted him to the point of committing unspeakable acts?

Chapter 44: Deliberation Room Dialogue

Inside the small, windowless room, the jury gathered around a rectangular table. The atmosphere was tense, the weight of responsibility hanging heavily in the air. Twelve individuals, each with their own perspectives and biases, now held the fate of John MacGregor in their hands.

Jury Foreperson: (Clearing throat) Alright, everyone, let's get started. We have a serious decision to make.

Juror 1: (Frowning) Those images, though... I can't shake them from my mind.

Juror 2: (Nodding) It's hard to believe the guy we saw in court could do something like that.

Juror 3: (Squinting) We're not here to judge his character; we're here to determine his guilt.

Juror 4: (Sighing) But his mental state, that's crucial. The Defence made a compelling case.

Juror 5: (Shaking head) Still, he did what he did. How do we justify that?

Juror 6: (Leaning back) We need to separate our emotions from the facts. Was he in control of his actions?

Juror 7: (Frowning) That psychiatrist... they said he was dealing with PTSD. Could that really drive someone to such extremes?

Juror 8: (Crossing arms) I can't believe he didn't have any other option. Wasn't there a less brutal way to deal with whatever was bothering him?

Juror 9: (Looking thoughtful) But didn't the Defence argue that he felt a sense of duty, like he was helping society?

Juror 10: (Shrugging) Duty or not, there's no excuse for what he did.

Juror 11: (Rubbing temples) It's not black and white. We need to weigh the factors carefully.

Juror 12: (Tapping fingers) Let's take a vote. Guilty or not guilty?

The room fell silent as each juror contemplated their decision. The weight of the evidence, the haunting images, and the complex web of John's mental state played tug-of-war in their minds.

Jury Foreperson: (Collecting votes) All right, let's see where we stand.

The jury began the process of casting their votes, each slip of paper contributing to the unfolding verdict. John MacGregor's fate hung in the balance, the deliberation room holding the power to shape the remainder of his life.

Chapter 48: The Inked Tapestry

In the heart of Koh Tao, where the rhythmic melody of the sea and the vibrant hues of the sunset painted the backdrop, John MacGregor found solace in the art of tattooing. The inked tapestry of stories that unfolded under his skilled hands became more than just a livelihood; it was an expression of love and a celebration of the artistry he had cultivated over the years.

The whirr of the tattoo machine, the subtle sting of the needle, and the intricate dance of creativity filled John with a profound sense of purpose. Each design was a journey—an exploration of the human canvas that stretched beyond the physical into the realms of emotion and self-discovery.

For John, tattooing was more than a craft; it was a therapeutic process. As he etched stories onto the skin of his clients, he felt a connection, a shared narrative that transcended spoken words. His studio became a sanctuary, a space where people bared not only their skin but also their souls, seeking transformation, healing, or simply a beautiful mark to carry with them.

The island's vibrant energy and the diverse mix of clientele fuelled John's passion. From fellow travellers sharing tales of adventure to locals embracing tradition through ink, every session became a collaborative masterpiece—a fusion of artist and muse.

As the ink flowed and designs took shape, John found joy in the diversity of his creations. Marine motifs inspired by the island's rich aquatic life, intricate mandalas reflecting spiritual journeys, and symbols of personal significance adorned the bodies of those who entrusted him with their stories.

His studio became a hub of creativity and self-expression. The intoxicating scent of ink and the steady hum of the tattoo machine resonated with the rhythm of island life. The cash from the sale of his house in Nottingham provided not only financial stability but the freedom to immerse himself fully in his newfound paradise.

With each passing day, John realized that Koh Tao had become more than just an escape—it was a canvas for his second act. The love he poured into his craft and the connections he forged through ink transformed the quaint studio into a haven for those seeking not only art but a piece of the island's magic.

Under the tropical skies and amidst the turquoise waters, John MacGregor lived his dream, weaving stories into the inked tapestry of Koh Tao—a living testament to the transformative power of art and the boundless possibilities that unfold when one follows their passion.

Chapter 49: Thai Grass

The sweet aroma of the Thai breeze filled the air as John settled into his new life on Koh Toa. The island offered not only the tranquillity he sought but also unexpected connections. As he explored the community, he struck up an unlikely friendship with Pee Towi, the island's detective known for his laid-back demeanour.

One evening, Pee Towi invited John to a gathering at the mayor's residence. The mayor, a wise and weathered figure, had a penchant for cultivating the vibrant Thai grass that adorned the nearby island of Koh Phangan.

The group sat under the starlit sky, sharing stories and laughter. The mayor, with a twinkle in his eye, pointed to the lush greenery surrounding them. "This island provides us with many gifts," he said, his tone suggesting a deeper understanding.

John, intrigued by the camaraderie and the shared appreciation for the island's natural treasures, felt a sense of belonging he hadn't experienced in a long time. The mayor's wisdom, Pee Towy's amiable presence, and the gentle sway of the palm trees created an atmosphere of acceptance and understanding.

As they passed around a pipe loaded with the fragrant Thai grass, the group revelled in the simplicity of the moment. The mayor shared stories of the island's history and its unspoken agreements, emphasizing the importance of respecting the delicate balance of their shared paradise.

In this serene setting, John found a new chapter unfolding—one where the soothing rhythm of the waves and the camaraderie of his newfound friends replaced the chaos of his past.

Chapter 51: First Tattoo.

Laura, a traveller from Abu Dhabi, found herself drawn to the serene shores of Koh Tao, seeking not only the sun-kissed beaches but also a memento to immortalize her nomadic spirit. As she entered "Island Tattoos," the subtle aroma of saltwater and the rhythmic lull of the sea set the backdrop for a transformative experience.

John, the seasoned artist who had once navigated the tumultuous seas of his own past, welcomed Laura into his studio. Their conversation flowed seamlessly, like the waves that embraced the island's coastline. In sharing tales of distant deserts and bustling cityscapes, they forged a connection that transcended the confines of the small, seaside studio.

The design took shape—a fusion of Arabic calligraphy and abstract patterns, a visual representation of Laura's multicultural journey. Each stroke of the needle was imbued with intention, a bridge between her past and the untold adventures awaiting her.

As the tattoo machine hummed to life, the initial sting faded into a rhythmic dance between artist and canvas. Laura, resilient and unyielding, embraced the pain as a conduit for personal transformation. The sun dipped lower on the horizon, casting a warm glow over the evolving masterpiece.

The design, now etched onto Laura's skin, told a story only she could fully comprehend. It whispered of the scorching sands of the Arabian Desert, the vibrant souks of Abu Dhabi, and the unexplored paths that lay ahead. In that quiet studio by the sea, pain and pleasure coalesced into a singular moment of catharsis.

As the final touches were applied, John handed Laura a mirror. Her eyes met the reflection of a tapestry that encapsulated the essence of her adventurous soul. The pain, now a distant memory, had become an integral part of a visual memoir—a compass guiding her forward into the unknown, a testament to the transformative power of ink and introspection.

Chapter 52: Shadows of Sairee

The night air on Koh Tao was alive with the melodic rhythms of reggae, as the trio found themselves ensconced in the quaint embrace of the Reggae Bar. Andy, the Aussie proprietor, served up chilled drinks with a side of easy-going banter, creating an ambiance that invited both locals and travellers into its laid-back embrace.

As the evening unfolded, Laura's laughter and John's stories intertwined with the subtle notes of the music. Under the canopy of stars and swaying palms, a connection deeper than shared tales began to weave itself into the fabric of the night.

Amidst the laughter, the conversation took a turn toward the island's darker history—the haunting echoes of an incident that had left an indelible mark on Koh Tao. The murder of two British backpackers in 2014 on the pristine shores of Sairee Beach was a chilling tale that sent shivers through the spines of even the most carefree revellers.

John, his eyes gazing into the flickering flames of the beach bonfire, narrated the events with a sombre tone. The victims, David Miller and Hannah Witheridge, had been found lifeless on the sands, their dreams of adventure extinguished in an act of senseless violence.

The island's reputation had been tarnished, and the shadows of that tragedy lingered in the collective memory of those who called Koh Tao home. Rumours and speculations about the investigation's integrity and the reliability of the Thai justice system had become an inseparable part of the narrative.

Yet, as the three sat beneath the starlit sky, the weight of the past was momentarily lifted by the camaraderie of the present. The Reggae Bar, with its makeshift charm, stood as a testament to the island's ability to heal, to dance despite the shadows that clung to its history.

Laura, captivated by John's tales and the island's mystique, suggested a midnight stroll along Sairee Beach—an invitation laden with unspoken sentiments. The moonlit sands would bear witness to a chapter yet to unfold, where the ghosts of the past mingled with the promise of newfound connections under the tropical night sky.

Chapter 53: Moonlit Standoff

The moon cast its silvery glow upon Sairee Beach, turning the sands into an ethereal canvas where shadows danced in rhythm with the gentle waves. John and Laura strolled along the shoreline, their footsteps leaving imprints that the tide would soon erase. The rhythmic sound of the sea provided a soothing backdrop to their midnight escapade.

As they walked, wrapped in the tranquillity of the night, a solitary figure emerged from the shadows. The stranger's silhouette carved an imposing presence against the moonlit canvas. An uneasy tension filled the air as he began to approach, his steps purposeful and unsettling.

John, attuned to the subtle shifts in the atmosphere, tightened his grip on Laura's hand. The rhythmic lapping of the waves transformed into a heartbeat—a primal rhythm pulsating through the stillness. The stranger's intentions remained veiled in the obscurity of the night, but the tension escalated with each approaching step.

Laura, sensing the mounting unease, instinctively pulled closer to John, her eyes fixed on the stranger. A veil of caution fell over them, eclipsing the serenity of the beach. John's stance subtly shifted, a silent declaration that he would defend against any threat to the fragile peace they had found.

The stranger, catching the resolute gaze and unwavering stance of John, hesitated. A pregnant pause enveloped the beach, as if time itself held its breath. In that moment, Laura, feeling the tension, started to run, a burst of movement in the otherwise still night.

The stranger, observing John's steady posture and sensing no vulnerability in the face of confrontation, made a silent decision. He stopped in his tracks, choosing not to pursue the encounter further. Perhaps it was the strength emanating from John or the realization that this was not a confrontation he sought.

As Laura sprinted across the moonlit sands, the stranger watched for a moment, then turned and retreated into the shadows from whence he came. The beach, momentarily disturbed, resumed its nocturnal serenade—a symphony of sea whispers and distant melodies from the Reggae Bar.

John, his defensive stance relaxing, met Laura halfway. Their hearts, racing with the adrenaline of the encounter, gradually found the calming cadence of the ocean. The night, though briefly interrupted, resumed its enchantment as they continued their moonlit stroll—a couple, connected not just by shared tales but also by the unspoken understanding that in the face of shadows, they stood united.

Chapter 54: Tides of Passion

The night unfolded like a sultry dance, the air thick with the scent of the sea and the promise of something more. The beachside cabin, nestled amidst swaying palms, offered an intimate refuge from the moonlit world outside.

Inside, the air was heavy with the tropical humidity, and the soft glow of lanterns painted the room in warm hues. Laura's laughter echoed in harmony with the rhythmic cadence of the waves, creating a symphony of shared moments.

The heat of the night wrapped around them like a lover's embrace, making their skin glisten in the dim light. As they explored the contours of each other's bodies, the night became a canvas for passion—intense and consuming. The air hung with the intoxicating fragrance of desire, mingling with the salty sea breeze that whispered through the open windows.

Sweat, both from the humidity and the fervour of their connection, adorned their bodies like liquid diamonds, accentuating the shared journey of exploration. The bed, now a sanctuary for their tangled limbs, bore witness to the ebb and flow of passion—an intimate dance that mirrored the tides just beyond their haven.

In the hushed moments of reprieve, Laura's breathy admission lingered in the air. "I liked the thrill of it, you know," she confessed, her eyes gleaming with a mix of excitement and vulnerability. The encounter on the beach had ignited a flame within her, and in the afterglow of shared intimacy, confessions found a safe haven.

As dawn approached, they lay entwined, the sounds of the sea offering a lullaby to their tangled bodies. Laura, tracing patterns on John's chest, shared her dreams. "I've always wanted a full back tattoo," she confessed, her fingers dancing lightly over his skin. "Something intricate, something that tells a story."

A spark of enthusiasm lit up John's eyes. The prospect of such a monumental project intrigued him, the challenge of capturing a narrative within the inked tapestry of Laura's skin. "I can do that for you," he declared, a whisper of promise in his voice.

But he knew that such an endeavour required preparation. "I'll need to go to Singapore for more ink, a special blend," he explained, contemplating the artistic journey that awaited him.

Laura, basking in the post-passion glow, nodded in agreement. The promise of the inked narrative, an intimate collaboration between artist and canvas, added a layer of anticipation to the tender moments they had shared. As the first light of dawn kissed the horizon, they lay intertwined, their stories converging in the timeless embrace of the tropical night.

One evening, as the sun dipped below the horizon, casting hues of pink and orange across the ocean, John invited Laura to the studio. The ambiance was different this time—a blend of nervous excitement and a touch of mystery. Laura, unaware of the unfolding plan, entered the studio with a curious smile.

As they stood amidst the inked tapestry of the sea, John couldn't help but feel a sense of possessiveness. The vibrant tableau on Laura's back was not merely a piece of art; it held within it a piece of their shared experience; a fragment of time spent crafting stories with each stroke of the Knife.

"Close your eyes," John whispered to Laura, his voice carrying a blend of secrecy and excitement. She complied, trusting the artist who had transformed her skin into a living canvas.

Silence enveloped the room as John carefully worked, executing his plan with precision. When Laura opened her eyes, a mixture of awe and disbelief painted her face. Before her stood a framed piece, not of canvas or paper, but of inked skin—the very skin that had borne the tales of the sea.

Mounted in a custom frame, the tattooed skin became a work of art—a testament to the ephemeral nature of memory and the tangible embodiment of an intimate creation. The colours shimmered, capturing the essence of the sea, while the delicate lines formed a dance of turtles and coral. The framed tattoo, an unconventional masterpiece, hung on the studio wall, embodying a unique intersection of art, memory, and the ephemeral nature of their connection.

As the studio absorbed the presence of this unusual artwork, John couldn't help but smile. The canvas of memory, once etched on Laura's back, now adorned the studio—a symbol of their shared journey, a fragment of time suspended on the wall, and a reminder that art, in its myriad forms, could transcend the boundaries of convention.

Chapter 59: The Mystery Deepens

As questions arose about Laura's sudden absence, speculation buzzed through the small island community. Some believed she had returned to Abu Dhabi, as John had mentioned. Others thought she might have ventured to a neighbouring island for a solo adventure.

In the quaint island town, whispers and inquiries spread like wildfire. The local police caught wind of the curiosity surrounding Laura's whereabouts and began investigating. The framed tattoo in the studio became a focal point of intrigue, attracting both admiration and concern.

People, now with heightened interest, gathered at "Island Tattoos," each asking John the same question: "Where is Laura?" Yet, John, shrouded in mystery, only offered cryptic responses, adding fuel to the speculations surrounding the missing woman.

Rumours and uncertainty mounted, setting the stage for the unfolding drama on the serene shores of Koh Toa.

Chapter 60: Shadows of Inquiry

Amidst the flickering candlelight and the subtle fragrance of incense, John sat in front of the framed tattoo, contemplating the series of events that led to this moment. His emotions oscillated between a sense of accomplishment and a lingering void left by Laura's absence.

As the shrine-like setup surrounded the masterpiece, the air was thick with a mix of reverence and secrecy. The police from the mainland, curious about the rumours surrounding Laura, arrived on the island. Detectives, accompanied by the local authorities, sought answers to the mysterious circumstances surrounding her sudden departure.

The studio, once a haven for creativity, now held an air of tension as the police began their questioning. The islanders, fuelled by local gossip, observed the scene with a mix of concern and fascination. John, the enigmatic artist, faced the inquiries with a stoic demeanour, revealing little about the events that transpired.

The chapter unfolds with a dance of shadows and whispers, as the police attempt to unravel the truth hidden within the inked masterpiece and the enigmatic tale of Laura's disappearance.

Chapter 61: A Foreign Justice

The wheels of Thai justice turned with a rhythm unfamiliar to John. Arrested on suspicion of Laura Turner's murder, he found himself navigating a legal landscape vastly different from the one he knew in the UK. The Thai detectives, stern-faced and resolute, escorted him off the island, the whispers of the locals blending with the distant waves.

In Bangkok, a bustling metropolis pulsating with life, John was assigned an English representative to serve as a bridge between him and the intricacies of the Thai legal system. The representative, well-versed in the complexities of foreign involvement in Thai cases, explained the gravity of the situation.

As his case made its way through the Thai legal apparatus, the stark differences in legal proceedings became apparent. In Thailand, the rules for foreigners, or 'Farang' as they were colloquially known, diverged from those applied to locals. The cultural nuances, language barriers, and idiosyncrasies of Thai law added layers of complexity to John's predicament.

As the English representative worked to navigate the foreigner through the labyrinthine legal process, John grappled with uncertainty about his fate. The chapter unfolds against the backdrop of Bangkok's bustling streets, where tuk-tuks weaved through traffic, and the humid air bore witness to a legal drama that transcended borders.

Chapter 62: Confronting the Abyss

The looming presence of the 'Bangkok Hilton,' a moniker locals bestowed upon the notorious Bangkok Central Prison, cast a shadow over John's fate. As he faced the prospect of confinement within its walls, he understood that survival would become a daily battle. The British government's support seemed distant, leaving him to navigate the labyrinthine Thai penal system alone.

Entering the notorious prison felt like crossing into another realm. The acrid scent of despair lingered in the air as iron bars clanged shut behind him. The cacophony of distant voices, cries, and the occasional harsh command echoed through the cold, dimly lit corridors.

In the confines of his cell, the reality of his situation sank in. The Bangkok Hilton was a place where the fight for survival extended beyond the legal battles. It was a microcosm of its own, where alliances and conflicts formed between inmates, and where the concept of justice often took on a twisted form.

As the days turned into nights within the unforgiving walls, John steeled himself for the challenges ahead. The underworld of the prison, with its unwritten rules and hierarchies, awaited him. The prospect of enduring this harsh environment, often depicted in ominous hues by fellow inmates, kindled a fire within him. It wasn't just a physical fight; it was a battle for his sanity, identity, and the will to endure the consequences of his actions.

This chapter unfolds against the backdrop of the gritty reality inside the Bangkok Hilton, where survival becomes an art, and resilience a currency. John MacGregor, a foreigner navigating the harsh realm of the Thai prison system, confronts the abyss that awaits him, determined to emerge from its depths unbroken.

Chapter 63: The Art of Survival

In the belly of the Bangkok Hilton, John MacGregor weathered the initial storms of brutality. The first few months blurred into a painful collage of beatings and harsh realities. The confines of the prison walls became his daily battleground, and survival required adapting to the ruthless hierarchies that governed life inside.

Andy's unexpected act of solidarity, providing John with the basics of his tattoo gear, emerged as a lifeline amid the chaos. Armed with his skilful hands and the promise of indelible ink, John found a precarious foothold within the intricate social fabric of the prison. Inmates, seeking an escape from their grim surroundings, offered Favors in exchange for the transformative power of a tattoo.

As the news of John's plight reverberated across the UK, the public became voyeurs to his struggle. Each television broadcast and newspaper article transformed him into a symbol – a fallen countryman navigating the unforgiving corridors of a foreign penal system. Opinions ranged from sympathy to condemnation, shaping the narrative of a man who had ventured far from the familiar streets of Nottingham.

Back home, conversations about John's fate permeated living rooms and pubs, creating a dissonant chorus of judgment and speculation. His story became a national discourse, a lens through which people examined their own beliefs about justice, morality, and the limits of empathy.

Inside the prison, John etched tattoos that told stories of resilience and defiance on the bodies of his fellow inmates. In the midst of brutality, he found solace in the rhythmic buzz of his tattoo machine, each stroke a testament to the indomitable spirit that refused to be extinguished.

This chapter delves into John's adaptation to the harsh realities of prison life, where survival takes on many forms, and the artistry of tattooing becomes a powerful currency in the quest for resilience. The narrative unfolds against the backdrop of a divided public opinion, shaping the trajectory of John MacGregor's odyssey through the depths of the Bangkok Hilton.

Chapter 64 The Abyss Beckons

Inside the unforgiving confines of the Bangkok Hilton, John MacGregor's struggle for survival took a darker turn. Despite his tattooing skills garnering him a degree of protection, the brutal realities of the prison continued to exact a heavy toll. The UK government's attempts to negotiate his release faced insurmountable obstacles within the Thai legal system.

As the public back home moved on to the next sensational story, John MacGregor's fate became a forgotten footnote in the annals of international misadventure. The Bangkok Hilton, with its oppressive silence and looming shadows, became the final canvas for his tale. The harsh realities of prison life, coupled with the demons of his own past, gradually consumed him.

THE END

.

Printed in Great Britain
by Amazon

41537702R00030